D1335228

Stories

to

Share

at

Christmas

Published in the UK by Scholastic Children's Books, 2020
Euston House, 24 Eversholt Street, London, NW1 1DB
A division of Scholastic Limited

London – New York – Toronto – Sydney – Auckland
Mexico City – New Delhi – Hong Kong

SCHOLASTIC and associated logos are trademarks and/or
registered trademarks of Scholastic Inc.

This collection first published in 2016 as *Christmas Stories*.

Story introduction text copyright © Scholastic Ltd, 2016
Cover art © David Wardle, 2020

ISBN 978 0702 30479 8

A CIP catalogue record for this book is available from the British Library.

Printed by CPI Group (UK) Ltd, Croydon, CR0 4YY
Papers used by Scholastic Children's Books are made
from wood grown in sustainable forests.

1 3 5 7 9 10 8 6 4 2

www.scholastic.co.uk

Stories

to

Share

at

Christmas

SCHOLASTIC

Contents

"A Merry Christmas"
from *Little Women* by Louisa May Alcott

Little Women is Louisa May Alcott's classic tale of the four March sisters – Meg, Jo, Beth and Amy – growing up in 19th century America. Appropriately for the season, the book contains strong Christian themes of selflessness and charity.

As the book begins, the formerly wealthy March family have fallen on hard times. "It's so dreadful to be poor!" laments Meg, while Jo complains that, "Christmas won't be Christmas without any presents." To cheer themselves up, they decide to spend what little money they have on things for themselves. But soon the spirit of generosity overcomes them and they choose instead to buy gifts for their poor mother.

Adding to their woes is the fact that their father is off participating in the Civil War that was threatening to tear apart the United States at the time the story was set. But the girls receive a letter from him reminding them to be good and to work hard, which makes them ashamed of their earlier selfishness.

In this newly generous spirit, they awaken on Christmas morning, and soon discover that doing nice things for those less fortunate than themselves makes for a truly rewarding Christmas.

Jo was the first to wake in the grey dawn of Christmas morning. No stockings hung at the fireplace, and for a moment she felt as much disappointed as she did long ago, when her little sock fell down because it was so crammed with goodies. Then she remembered her mother's promise, and, slipping her hand under her pillow, drew out a little crimson-covered book. She knew it very well, for it was that beautiful old story of the best life ever lived, and Jo felt that it was a true guidebook for any pilgrim going the long journey. She woke Meg with a "Merry Christmas," and bade her see what was under her pillow. A green-covered book appeared, with the same picture inside, and a few words written by their mother, which made their one present very precious in their eyes. Presently Beth and Amy woke, to rummage and find their little books also – one dove-coloured, the other blue; and all sat looking at and talking about them, while the east grew rosy with the coming day.

In spite of her small vanities, Margaret had a sweet and pious nature, which unconsciously influenced her sisters, especially Jo, who loved her very tenderly, and obeyed her because her advice was so gently given.

"Girls," said Meg seriously, looking from the tumbled head beside her to the two little night-capped ones in the room beyond, "mother wants us to read and love and mind these books, and we must begin at once. We used to be faithful about it; but since father went away, and all this war trouble unsettled us, we have neglected many things. You can do as you please; but I shall keep my book on the table here, and read a little every morning as soon as I wake, for I know it will do me good, and help me through the day."

Then she opened her new book and began to read. Jo put her arm round her, and, leaning cheek to cheek, read also, with the quiet expression so seldom seen on her restless face.

"How good Meg is! Come, Amy, let's do as they do. I'll help you with the hard words, and they'll explain things if we don't understand," whispered Beth, very much impressed by the pretty books and her sisters' example.

"I'm glad mine is blue," said Amy; and then the rooms were very still while the pages were softly turned, and the winter sunshine crept in to touch the bright heads and serious faces with a Christmas greeting.

"Where is mother?" asked Meg, as she and Jo ran down to thank her for their gifts, half an hour later.

"Goodness only knows. Some poor creeter come a-beggin', and your ma went straight off to see what was needed. There never *was* such a woman for givin' away vittles and drink, clothes and firin'," replied Hannah, who had lived with the family since Meg was born, and was considered by them all more as a friend than a servant.

"She will be back soon, I think; so fry your cakes, and have everything ready," said Meg, looking over the presents which were collected in a basket and kept under the sofa, ready to be produced at the proper time. "Why, where is Amy's bottle of cologne?" she added, as the little flask did not appear.

"She took it out a minute ago, and went off with it to put a ribbon on it, or some such notion," replied Jo, dancing about the room to take the first stiffness off the new army-slippers.

"How nice my handkerchiefs look, don't they? Hannah washed and ironed them for me, and I marked them all myself," said Beth, looking proudly at the somewhat uneven letters which had cost her such labour.

"Bless the child! she's gone and put 'Mother' on them instead of 'M. March.' How funny!" cried Jo, taking up one.

"Isn't it right? I thought it was better to do it so, because Meg's initials are 'M.M.,' and I don't want anyone to use these but Marmee," said Beth, looking troubled.

"It's all right, dear, and a very pretty idea – quite sensible, too, for no one can ever mistake now. It will please her very much, I know," said Meg, with a frown for Jo and a smile for Beth.

"There's mother. Hide the basket, quick!" cried Jo, as a door slammed, and steps sounded in the hall.

Amy came in hastily, and looked rather abashed when she saw her sisters all waiting for her.

"Where have you been, and what are you hiding behind you?" asked Meg, surprised to see, by her hood and cloak, that lazy Amy had been out so early.

"Don't laugh at me, Jo! I didn't mean anyone should know till the time came. I only meant to change the little bottle for a big one, and I gave *all* my money to get it, and I'm truly trying not to be selfish any more."

As she spoke, Amy showed the handsome flask which replaced the cheap one; and looked so earnest and humble in her little effort to forget herself that Meg hugged her on the spot, and Jo pronounced her "a trump," while Beth ran to the window, and picked her finest rose to ornament the stately bottle.

"You see I felt ashamed of my present, after reading and talking about being good this morning, so I ran round the corner and changed it the minute I was up: and I'm *so* glad, for mine is the handsomest now."

Another bang of the street-door sent the basket under the sofa, and the girls to the table, eager for breakfast.

"Merry Christmas, Marmee! Many of them! Thank you for our books; we read some, and mean to every day," they cried, in chorus.

"Merry Christmas, little daughters! I'm glad you began at once, and hope you will keep on. But I want to say one word before we sit down. Not far away from here lies a poor woman with a little newborn baby. Six children are huddled into one bed to keep from freezing, for they have no fire. There is nothing to eat over there; and the oldest boy came to tell me they were suffering hunger and cold. My girls, will you give them your breakfast as a Christmas present?"

They were all unusually hungry, having waited nearly an hour, and for a minute no one spoke; only a minute, for Jo exclaimed impetuously:

"I'm so glad you came before we began!"

"May I go and help carry the things to the poor little children?" asked Beth, eagerly.

"*I* shall take the cream and the muffins," added Amy, heroically giving up the articles she most liked.

Meg was already covering the buckwheats, and piling the bread into one big plate.

"I thought you'd do it," said Mrs March, smiling as if satisfied. "You shall all go and help me, and when we come back we will have bread and milk for breakfast, and make it up at dinnertime."

They were soon ready, and the procession set out. Fortunately it was early, and they went through back streets, so few people saw them, and no one laughed at the queer party.

A poor, bare, miserable room it was, with broken windows, no fire, ragged bed-clothes, a sick mother, wailing baby, and a group of pale, hungry children cuddled under one old quilt, trying to keep warm.

How the big eyes stared and the blue lips smiled as the girls went in!

"Ach, mein Gott! it is good angels come to us!" said the poor woman, crying for joy.

"Funny angels in hoods and mittens," said Jo, and set them laughing.

In a few minutes it really did seem as if kind spirits had been at work there. Hannah, who had carried wood, made a fire, and stopped up the broken panes with old hats and her own cloak. Mrs March gave the mother tea and gruel, and comforted her with promises of help, while she dressed the little baby as tenderly as if it had been her own. The girls, meantime, spread the table, set the children round the fire, and fed them like so many hungry birds – laughing, talking, and trying to understand the funny broken English.

"Das ist gut!" "Die Engel-kinder!" cried the poor things, as they ate, and warmed their purple hands at the comfortable blaze.

The girls had never been called angel children before, and thought it very agreeable, especially Jo, who had been considered a "Sancho" ever since she was born. That was a very happy breakfast, though they didn't get any of it; and when they went away, leaving comfort behind, I think there were not in all the city four merrier people than the hungry little girls who gave away their breakfasts and contented themselves with bread and milk on Christmas morning.

"That's loving our neighbour better than ourselves, and I like it," said Meg, as they set out their presents, while their mother was upstairs collecting clothes for the poor Hummels.

Not a very splendid show, but there was a great deal of love done up in the few little bundles; and the tall vase of red roses, white chrysanthemums, and trailing vines, which stood in the middle, gave quite an elegant air to the table.

"She's coming! Strike up, Beth! Open the door, Amy! Three cheers for Marmee!" cried Jo, prancing about, while Meg went to conduct mother to the seat of honour.

Beth played her gayest march, Amy threw open the door, and Meg enacted escort with great dignity. Mrs March was both surprised and touched; and smiled with her eyes full as she examined her presents, and read the little notes which accompanied them. The slippers went on at once, a new handkerchief was slipped into her pocket, well scented with Amy's cologne, the rose was fastened in her bosom, and the nice gloves were pronounced a "perfect fit."

There was a good deal of laughing and kissing and explaining, in the simple, loving fashion which makes these home-festivals so pleasant at the time, so sweet to remember long afterward, and then all fell to work.

The morning charities and ceremonies took so much time that the rest of the day was devoted to preparations for the evening festivities. Being still too young to go often to the theatre, and not rich enough to afford any great outlay for private performances, the girls put their wits to work, and – necessity being the mother of invention – made whatever they needed. Very clever were some of their productions – pasteboard guitars, antique lamps made of old-fashioned butter-boats covered with silver paper, gorgeous robes of old cotton, glittering with tin spangles from a pickle factory, and armour covered with the same useful diamond-shaped bits, left in sheets when the lids of tin preserve-pots were cut out. The furniture was used to being turned topsy-turvy, and the big chamber was the scene of many innocent revels.

No gentlemen were admitted; so Jo played male parts to her heart's content, and took immense satisfaction in a pair of russet-leather boots given her by a friend, who knew a lady who knew an actor. These boots, an old foil, and a slashed doublet once used by an artist for some picture, were Jo's chief treasures, and appeared on all occasions. The smallness of the company made it necessary for the two principal actors to take several parts apiece; and they certainly deserved some credit for the hard work they did in learning three or four different parts, whisking in and out of various costumes, and managing the stage besides. It was excellent drill for their memories, a harmless amusement, and employed many hours which otherwise would have been idle, lonely, or spent in less profitable society.

On Christmas night, a dozen girls piled on to the bed which was the dress-circle, and sat before the blue and yellow chintz curtains in a most flattering state of expectancy. There was a good deal of rustling and whispering behind the curtain, a trifle of lamp-smoke, and an occasional giggle from Amy, who was apt to get hysterical in the excitement of the moment. Presently a bell sounded, the curtains flew apart, and the Operatic Tragedy began.

"A gloomy wood," according to the one play-bill, was represented by a few shrubs in pots, green baize on the floor, and a cave in the distance. This cave was made with a clothes-horse for a roof, bureaus for walls; and in it was a small furnace in full blast, with a black pot on it, and an old witch bending over it. The stage was dark, and the glow of the furnace had a fine effect, especially as real steam issued from the kettle when the witch took off the cover. A moment was allowed for the first thrill to subside; then Hugo, the villain, stalked in with a clanking sword at his side, a slouched hat, black beard, mysterious cloak, and the boots. After pacing to and fro in much agitation, he struck his forehead, and burst out in a wild strain, singing of his hatred to Roderigo, his love for Zara, and his pleasing resolution to kill the one and win the other. The gruff tones of Hugo's voice, with an occasional shout when his feelings overcame him, were very impressive, and the audience applauded the moment he paused for breath. Bowing with the air of one accustomed to public praise, he stole to the cavern, and ordered Hagar to come forth with a commanding "What ho, minion! I need thee!"

Out came Meg, with grey horse-hair hanging about her face, a red and black robe, a staff, and cabalistic signs upon her cloak. Hugo demanded a potion to make Zara adore him, and one to destroy Roderigo.

Hagar, in a fine dramatic melody, promised both, and proceeded to call up the spirit who would bring the love philter:

> "Hither, hither, from thy home,
> Airy sprite, I bid thee come!
> Born of roses, fed on dew,
> Charms and potions canst thou brew?
> Bring me here, with elfin speed,
> The fragrant philter which I need;
> Make it sweet and swift and strong,
> Spirit, answer now my song!"

A soft strain of music sounded, and then at the back of the cave appeared a little figure in cloudy white, with glittering wings, golden hair, and a garland of roses on its head. Waving a wand, it sang:

> "Hither I come,
> From my airy home,
> Afar in the silver moon.
> Take the magic spell,
> And use it well,
> Or its power will vanish soon!"

And, dropping a small, gilded bottle at the witch's feet, the spirit vanished. Another chant from Hagar produced another apparition – not a lovely one; for, with a bang, an ugly black imp appeared, and, having croaked a reply, tossed a dark bottle at Hugo, and disappeared with a mocking laugh. Having warbled his thanks and put the potions in his boots, Hugo departed; and Hagar informed the audience that, as he had killed a few of her friends in times past, she has cursed him, and intends to thwart his plans, and be revenged on him. Then the curtain fell, and the audience reposed and ate candy while discussing the merits of the play.

A good deal of hammering went on before the curtain rose again; but when it became evident what a masterpiece of stage-carpentering had been got up, no one murmured at the delay. It was truly superb! A tower rose to the ceiling; halfway up appeared a window, with a lamp burning at it, and behind the white curtain appeared Zara in a lovely blue and silver dress, waiting for Roderigo. He came in gorgeous array, with plumed cap, red cloak, chestnut love-locks, a guitar, and the boots, of course. Kneeling at the foot of the tower, he sang a serenade in melting tones. Zara replied, and, after a musical dialogue, consented to fly. Then came the grand effect of the play. Roderigo produced a rope-ladder, with five steps to it, threw up one end, and invited Zara to descend. Timidly she crept from her lattice, put her hand on Roderigo's shoulder, and was about to leap gracefully down, when, "Alas! alas for Zara!" she forgot her train – it caught in the window; the tower tottered, leaned forward, fell with a crash, and buried the unhappy lovers in the ruins!

A universal shriek arose as the russet boots waved wildly from the wreck, and a golden head emerged, exclaiming, "I told you so! I told you so!" With wonderful presence of mind, Don Pedro, the cruel sire, rushed in, dragged out his daughter, with a hasty aside:

"Don't laugh! Act as if it was all right!" – and, ordering Roderigo up, banished him from the kingdom with wrath and scorn. Though decidedly shaken by the fall of the tower upon him, Roderigo defied the old gentleman, and refused to stir. This dauntless example fired Zara: she also defied her sire, and he ordered them both to the deepest dungeons of the castle. A stout little retainer came in with chains, and led them away, looking very much frightened, and evidently forgetting the speech he ought to have made.

Act third was the castle hall; and here Hagar appeared, having come to free the lovers and finish Hugo. She hears him coming, and hides; sees him put the potions into two cups of wine, and bid the timid little servant "Bear them to the captives in their cells, and tell them I shall come anon." The servant takes Hugo aside to tell him something, and Hagar changes the cups for two others which are harmless. Ferdinando, the "minion," carries them away, and Hagar puts back the cup which holds the poison meant for Roderigo. Hugo, getting thirsty after a long warble, drinks it, loses his wits, and, after a good deal of clutching and stamping, falls flat and dies; while Hagar informs him what she has done in a song of exquisite power and melody.

This was a truly thrilling scene, though some persons might have thought that the sudden tumbling down of a quantity of long hair rather marred the effect of the villain's death. He was called before the curtain, and with great propriety appeared, leading Hagar, whose singing was considered more wonderful than all the rest of the performance put together.

Act fourth displayed the despairing Roderigo on the point of stabbing himself, because he has been told that Zara has deserted him. Just as the dagger is at his heart, a lovely song is sung under his window, informing him that Zara is true, but in danger, and he can save her, if he will. A key is thrown in, which unlocks the door, and in a spasm of rapture he tears off his chains, and rushes away to find and rescue his lady-love.

Act fifth opened with a stormy scene between Zara and Don Pedro. He wishes her to go into a convent, but she won't hear of it; and, after a touching appeal, is about to faint, when Roderigo dashes in and demands her hand. Don Pedro refuses, because he is not rich. They shout and gesticulate tremendously, but cannot agree, and Roderigo is about to bear away the exhausted Zara, when the timid servant enters with a letter and a bag from Hagar, who has mysteriously disappeared. The latter informs the party that she bequeaths untold wealth to the young pair, and an awful doom to Don Pedro, if he doesn't make them happy. The bag is opened, and several quarts of tin money shower down upon the stage, till it is quite glorified with the glitter. This entirely softens the "stern sire": he consents without a murmur, all join in a joyful chorus, and the curtain falls upon the lovers kneeling to receive Don Pedro's blessing in attitudes of the most romantic grace.

Tumultuous applause followed, but received an

unexpected check; for the cot-bed, on which the "dress-circle" was built, suddenly shut up, and extinguished the enthusiastic audience. Roderigo and Don Pedro flew to the rescue, and all were taken out unhurt, though many were speechless with laughter. The excitement had hardly subsided, when Hannah appeared, with "Mrs March's compliments, and would the ladies walk down to supper."

This was a surprise, even to the actors; and, when they saw the table, they looked at one another in rapturous amazement. It was like Marmee to get up a little treat for them; but anything so fine as this was unheard-of since the departed days of plenty. There was ice-cream – actually two dishes of it, pink and white – and cake and fruit and distracting French bonbons, and, in the middle of the table, four great bouquets of hothouse flowers!

It quite took their breath away; and they stared first at the table and then at their mother, who looked as if she enjoyed it immensely.

"Is it fairies?" asked Amy,

"It's Santa Claus," said Beth.

"Mother did it"; and Meg smiled her sweetest, in spite of her grey beard and white eyebrows.

"Aunt March had a good fit, and sent the supper," cried Jo, with a sudden inspiration.

"All wrong. Old Mr Laurence sent it," replied Mrs March.

"The Laurence boy's grandfather! What in the world put such a thing into his head? We don't know him!" exclaimed Meg.

"Hannah told one of his servants about your breakfast party. He is an odd old gentleman, but that pleased him. He knew my father, years ago; and he sent me a polite note this afternoon, saying he hoped I would allow him to express his friendly feeling toward my children by sending them a few trifles in honour of the day. I could not refuse; and so you have a little feast at night to make up for the bread-and-milk breakfast."

"That boy put it into his head, I know he did! He's a capital fellow, and I wish we could get acquainted. He looks as if he'd like to know us; but he's bashful, and Meg is so prim she won't let me speak to him when we pass," said Jo, as the plates went round, and the ice began to melt out of sight, with "Ohs!" and "Ahs!" of satisfaction.

"You mean the people who live in the big house next door, don't you?" asked one of the girls. "My mother knows old Mr Laurence; but says he's very proud, and doesn't like to mix with his neighbours. He keeps his grandson shut up, when he isn't riding or walking with his tutor, and makes him study very hard. We invited him to our party, but he didn't come. Mother says he's very nice, though he never speaks to us girls."

"Our cat ran away once, and he brought her back, and we talked over the fence, and were getting on capitally – all about cricket, and so on – when he saw Meg coming, and walked off. I mean to know him some day; for he needs fun, I'm sure he does," said Jo decidedly.

"I like his manners, and he looks like a little gentleman; so I've no objection to your knowing him, if a proper opportunity comes. He brought the flowers himself; and I should have asked him in, if I had been sure what was going on upstairs. He looked so wistful as he went away, hearing the frolic, and evidently having none of his own."

"It's a mercy you didn't, mother!" laughed Jo, looking at her boots. "But we'll have another play, some time, that he *can* see. Perhaps he'll help act; wouldn't that be jolly?"

"I never had such a fine bouquet before! How pretty it is!" And Meg examined her flowers with great interest.

"They *are* lovely! But Beth's roses are sweeter to me," said Mrs March, smelling the half-dead posy in her belt.

Beth nestled up to her, and whispered softly, "I wish I could send my bunch to father. I'm afraid he isn't having such a merry Christmas as we are."

"The Story of the Goblins Who Stole a Sexton"
from *The Pickwick Papers*
by Charles Dickens

There can be few authors with a greater claim to the Christmas season than Charles Dickens. To some he is considered "the man who invented Christmas", and books such as *A Christmas Carol* and *The Haunted Man* did much to popularize the traditions of the season.

First published in instalments between 1836 and 1837, Dickens' first novel, *The Pickwick Papers*, shows that Christmas was important to the author from the very beginning of his career. The book recounts a series of adventures by the members of the Pickwick Club, who are known as "Pickwickians".

Before the following extract begins, the Pickwickians have journeyed to the farm of Mr Wardle, and are celebrating the season with games, dancing, feasting and storytelling.

In this mood, Mr Wardle is encouraged to tell them the story of Gabriel Grub, an old sexton – which is a person who looks after graveyards – who was carried away by goblins one Christmas eve.

"In an old abbey town, down in this part of the country, a long, long while ago – so long, that the story must be a true one, because our great-grandfathers implicitly believed it – there officiated as sexton and grave-digger in the churchyard, one Gabriel Grub. It by no means follows that because a man is a sexton, and constantly surrounded by the emblems of mortality, therefore he should be a morose and melancholy man; your undertakers are the merriest fellows in the world; and I once had the honour of being on intimate terms with a mute, who in private life, and off duty, was as comical and jocose a little fellow as ever chirped out a devil-may-care song, without a hitch in his memory, or drained off a good stiff glass without stopping for breath. But notwithstanding these precedents to the contrary, Gabriel Grub was an ill-conditioned, cross-grained, surly fellow – a morose and lonely man, who consorted with nobody but himself, and an old wicker bottle which fitted into his large deep waistcoat pocket – and who eyed each merry face, as it passed him by, with such a deep scowl of malice and ill-humour, as it was difficult to meet without feeling something the worse for.

"A little before twilight one Christmas Eve, Gabriel shouldered his spade, lighted his lantern, and betook himself towards the old churchyard; for he had got a grave to finish by next morning, and, feeling very low, he thought it might raise his spirits, perhaps, if he went on with his work at once. As he went his way, up the ancient street, he saw the cheerful light of the blazing fires gleam through the old casements, and heard the loud laugh and the cheerful shouts of those who were assembled around them; he marked the bustling preparations for next day's cheer, and smelled the numerous savoury odours consequent thereupon, as they steamed up from the kitchen windows in clouds. All this was gall and wormwood to the heart of Gabriel Grub; and when groups of children bounded out of the houses, tripped across the road, and were met, before they could knock at the opposite door, by half a dozen curly-headed little rascals who crowded round them as they flocked upstairs to spend the evening in their Christmas games, Gabriel smiled grimly, and clutched the handle of his spade with a firmer grasp, as he thought of measles, scarlet fever, thrush, whooping-cough, and a good many other sources of consolation besides.

"In this happy frame of mind, Gabriel strode along, returning a short, sullen growl to the good-humoured greetings of such of his neighbours as now and then passed him, until he turned into the dark lane which led to the churchyard. Now, Gabriel had been looking forward to reaching the dark lane, because it was, generally speaking, a nice, gloomy, mournful place, into which the townspeople did not much care to go, except in broad daylight, and when the sun was shining; consequently, he was not a little indignant to hear a young urchin roaring out some jolly song about a merry Christmas, in this very sanctuary which had been called Coffin Lane ever since the days of the old abbey, and the time of the shaven-headed monks. As Gabriel walked on, and the voice drew nearer, he found it proceeded from a small boy, who was hurrying along, to join one of the little parties in the old street, and who, partly to keep himself company, and partly to prepare himself for the occasion, was shouting out the song at the highest pitch of his lungs. So Gabriel waited until the boy came up, and then dodged him into a corner, and rapped him over the head with his lantern five or six times, just to teach him to modulate his voice. And as the boy hurried away with his hand to his head, singing quite a different sort of tune, Gabriel Grub chuckled very heartily to himself, and entered the churchyard, locking the gate behind him.

"He took off his coat, set down his lantern, and getting into the unfinished grave, worked at it for an hour or so with right good-will. But the earth was hardened with the frost, and it was no very easy matter to break it up, and shovel it out; and although there was a moon, it was a very young one, and shed little light upon the grave, which was in the shadow of the church. At any other time, these obstacles would have made Gabriel Grub very moody and miserable, but he was so well pleased with having stopped the small boy's singing, that he took little heed of the scanty progress he had made, and looked down into the grave, when he had finished work for the night, with grim satisfaction, murmuring as he gathered up his things:

> Brave lodgings for one, brave lodgings for
>   one,
> A few feet of cold earth, when life is done;
> A stone at the head, a stone at the feet,
> A rich, juicy meal for the worms to eat;
> Rank grass overhead, and damp clay
>   around,
> Brave lodgings for one, these, in holy
>   ground!

"'Ho! ho!' laughed Gabriel Grub, as he sat himself down on a flat tombstone which was a favourite resting-place of his, and drew forth his wicker bottle. 'A coffin at Christmas! A Christmas box! Ho! ho! ho!'

"'Ho! ho! ho!' repeated a voice which sounded close behind him.

"Gabriel paused, in some alarm, in the act of raising the wicker bottle to his lips, and looked round. The bottom of the oldest grave about him was not more still and quiet than the churchyard in the pale moonlight. The cold hoar frost glistened on the tombstones, and sparkled like rows of gems, among the stone carvings of the old church. The snow lay hard and crisp upon the ground; and spread over the thickly-strewn mounds of earth, so white and smooth a cover that it seemed as if corpses lay there, hidden only by their winding sheets. Not the faintest rustle broke the profound tranquillity of the solemn scene. Sound itself appeared to be frozen up, all was so cold and still.

"'It was the echoes,' said Gabriel Grub, raising the bottle to his lips again.

"'It was *not*,' said a deep voice.

"Gabriel started up, and stood rooted to the spot with astonishment and terror; for his eyes rested on a form that made his blood run cold.

"Seated on an upright tombstone, close to him, was a strange, unearthly figure, whom Gabriel felt at once, was no being of this world. His long, fantastic legs which might have reached the ground, were cocked up, and crossed after a quaint, fantastic fashion; his sinewy arms were bare; and his hands rested on his knees. On his short, round body, he wore a close covering, ornamented with small slashes; a short cloak dangled at his back; the collar was cut into curious peaks, which served the goblin in lieu of ruff or neckerchief; and his shoes curled up at his toes into long points. On his head, he wore a broad-brimmed sugar-loaf hat, garnished with a single feather. The hat was covered with the white frost; and the goblin looked as if he had sat on the same tombstone very comfortably, for two or three hundred years. He was sitting perfectly still; his tongue was put out, as if in derision; and he was grinning at Gabriel Grub with such a grin as only a goblin could call up.

"'It was *not* the echoes,' said the goblin.

"Gabriel Grub was paralysed, and could make no reply.

"'What do you do here on Christmas Eve?' said the goblin sternly.

"'I came to dig a grave, Sir,' stammered Gabriel Grub.

"'What man wanders among graves and churchyards on such a night as this?' cried the goblin.

"'Gabriel Grub! Gabriel Grub!' screamed a wild chorus of voices that seemed to fill the churchyard. Gabriel looked fearfully round – nothing was to be seen.

"'What have you got in that bottle?' said the goblin.

"'Hollands, sir,' replied the sexton, trembling more than ever; for he had bought it of the smugglers, and he thought that perhaps his questioner might be in the excise department of the goblins.

"'Who drinks Hollands alone, and in a churchyard, on such a night as this?' said the goblin.

"'Gabriel Grub! Gabriel Grub!' exclaimed the wild voices again.

"The goblin leered maliciously at the terrified sexton, and then raising his voice, exclaimed:

"'And who, then, is our fair and lawful prize?'

"To this inquiry the invisible chorus replied, in a strain that sounded like the voices of many choristers singing to the mighty swell of the old church organ – a strain that seemed borne to the sexton's ears upon a wild wind, and to die away as it passed onward; but the burden of the reply was still the same, 'Gabriel Grub! Gabriel Grub!'

"The goblin grinned a broader grin than before, as he said, 'Well, Gabriel, what do you say to this?'

"The sexton gasped for breath.

"'What do you think of this, Gabriel?' said the goblin, kicking up his feet in the air on either side of the tombstone, and looking at the turned-up points with as much complacency as if he had been contemplating the most fashionable pair of Wellingtons in all Bond Street.

"'It's – it's – very curious, Sir,' replied the sexton, half dead with fright; 'very curious, and very pretty, but I think I'll go back and finish my work, Sir, if you please.'

"'Work!' said the goblin, 'what work?'

"'The grave, Sir; making the grave,' stammered the sexton.

"'Oh, the grave, eh?' said the goblin; 'who makes graves at a time when all other men are merry, and takes a pleasure in it?'

"Again the mysterious voices replied, 'Gabriel Grub! Gabriel Grub!'

"'I am afraid my friends want you, Gabriel,' said the goblin, thrusting his tongue farther into his cheek than ever – and a most astonishing tongue it was – 'I'm afraid my friends want you, Gabriel,' said the goblin.

"'Under favour, Sir,' replied the horror-stricken sexton, 'I don't think they can, Sir; they don't know me, Sir; I don't think the gentlemen have ever seen me, Sir.'

"'Oh, yes, they have,' replied the goblin; 'we know the man with the sulky face and grim scowl, that came down the street tonight, throwing his evil looks at the children, and grasping his burying-spade the tighter. We know the man who struck the boy in the envious malice of his heart, because the boy could be merry, and he could not. We know him, we know him.'

"Here, the goblin gave a loud, shrill laugh, which the echoes returned twentyfold; and throwing his legs up in the air, stood upon his head, or rather upon the very point of his sugar-loaf hat, on the narrow edge of the tombstone, whence he threw a Somerset with extraordinary agility, right to the sexton's feet, at which he planted himself in the attitude in which tailors generally sit upon the shop-board.

"'I – I – am afraid I must leave you, Sir,' said the sexton, making an effort to move.

"'Leave us!' said the goblin, 'Gabriel Grub going to leave us. Ho! ho! ho!'

"As the goblin laughed, the sexton observed, for one instant, a brilliant illumination within the windows of the church, as if the whole building were lighted up; it disappeared, the organ pealed forth a lively air, and whole troops of goblins, the very counterpart of the first one, poured into the churchyard, and began playing at leap-frog with the tombstones, never stopping for an instant to take breath, but 'overing' the highest among them, one after the other, with the most marvellous dexterity. The first goblin was a most astonishing leaper, and none of the others could come near him; even in the extremity of his terror the sexton could not help observing, that while his friends were content to leap over the common-sized gravestones, the first one took the family vaults, iron railings and all, with as much ease as if they had been so many street-posts.

"At last the game reached to a most exciting pitch; the organ played quicker and quicker, and the goblins leaped faster and faster, coiling themselves up, rolling head over heels upon the ground, and bounding over the tombstones like footballs. The sexton's brain whirled round with the rapidity of the motion he beheld, and his legs reeled beneath him, as the spirits flew before his eyes; when the goblin king, suddenly darting towards him, laid his hand upon his collar, and sank with him through the earth.

"When Gabriel Grub had had time to fetch his breath, which the rapidity of his descent had for the moment taken away, he found himself in what appeared to be a large cavern, surrounded on all sides by crowds of goblins, ugly and grim; in the centre of the room, on an elevated seat, was stationed his friend of the churchyard; and close behind him stood Gabriel Grub himself, without power of motion.

"'Cold tonight,' said the king of the goblins, 'very cold. A glass of something warm here!'

"At this command, half a dozen officious goblins, with a perpetual smile upon their faces, whom Gabriel

Grub imagined to be courtiers, on that account, hastily disappeared, and presently returned with a goblet of liquid fire, which they presented to the king.

"'Ah!' cried the goblin, whose cheeks and throat were transparent, as he tossed down the flame, 'this warms one, indeed! Bring a bumper of the same, for Mr Grub.'

"It was in vain for the unfortunate sexton to protest that he was not in the habit of taking anything warm at night; one of the goblins held him while another poured the blazing liquid down his throat; the whole assembly screeched with laughter, as he coughed and choked, and wiped away the tears which gushed plentifully from his eyes, after swallowing the burning draught.

"'And now,' said the king, fantastically poking the taper corner of his sugar-loaf hat into the sexton's eye, and thereby occasioning him the most exquisite pain; 'and now, show the man of misery and gloom, a few of the pictures from our own great storehouse!'

"As the goblin said this, a thick cloud which obscured the remoter end of the cavern rolled gradually away, and disclosed, apparently at a great distance, a small and scantily furnished, but neat and clean apartment. A crowd of little children were gathered round a bright fire, clinging to their mother's gown, and gambolling around her chair. The mother occasionally rose, and drew aside the window-curtain, as if to look for some expected object; a frugal meal was ready spread upon the table; and an elbow chair was placed near the fire. A knock was heard at the door; the mother opened it, and the children crowded round her, and clapped their hands for joy, as their father entered. He was wet and weary, and shook the snow from his garments, as the children crowded round him, and seizing his cloak, hat, stick, and gloves, with busy zeal, ran with them from the room. Then, as he sat down to his meal before the fire, the children climbed about his knee, and the mother sat by his side, and all seemed happiness and comfort.

"But a change came upon the view, almost imperceptibly. The scene was altered to a small bedroom, where the fairest and youngest child lay dying; the roses had fled from his cheek, and the light from his eye; and even as the sexton looked upon him with an interest he had never felt or known before, he died. His young brothers and sisters crowded round his little bed, and seized his tiny hand, so cold and heavy; but they shrank back from its touch, and looked with awe on his infant face; for calm and tranquil as it was, and sleeping in rest and peace as the beautiful child seemed to be, they saw that he was dead, and they knew that he was an angel looking down upon, and blessing them, from a bright and happy Heaven.

"Again the light cloud passed across the picture, and again the subject changed. The father and mother were old and helpless now, and the number of those about them was diminished more than half; but content and cheerfulness sat on every face, and beamed in every eye, as they crowded round the fireside, and told and listened to old stories of earlier and bygone days. Slowly and peacefully, the father sank into the grave, and, soon after, the sharer of all his cares and troubles followed him to a place of rest. The few who yet survived them, kneeled by their tomb, and watered the green turf which covered it with their tears; then rose, and turned away, sadly and mournfully, but not with bitter cries, or despairing lamentations, for they knew that they should one day meet again; and once more they mixed with the busy world, and their content and cheerfulness were restored. The cloud settled upon the picture, and concealed it from the sexton's view.

"'What do you think of *that*?' said the goblin, turning his large face towards Gabriel Grub.

"Gabriel murmured out something about its being

very pretty, and looked somewhat ashamed, as the goblin bent his fiery eyes upon him.

"'*You* a miserable man!' said the goblin, in a tone of excessive contempt. 'You!' He appeared disposed to add more, but indignation choked his utterance, so he lifted up one of his very pliable legs, and, flourishing it above his head a little, to insure his aim, administered a good sound kick to Gabriel Grub; immediately after which, all the goblins in waiting crowded round the wretched sexton, and kicked him without mercy, according to the established and invariable custom of courtiers upon earth, who kick whom royalty kicks, and hug whom royalty hugs.

"'Show him some more!' said the king of the goblins.

"At these words, the cloud was dispelled, and a rich and beautiful landscape was disclosed to view – there is just such another, to this day, within half a mile of the old abbey town. The sun shone from out the clear blue sky, the water sparkled beneath his rays, and the trees looked greener, and the flowers more gay, beneath its cheering influence. The water rippled on with a pleasant sound, the trees rustled in the light wind that murmured among their leaves, the birds sang upon the boughs, and the lark carolled on high her welcome to the morning. Yes, it was morning; the bright, balmy morning of summer; the minutest leaf, the smallest blade of grass, was instinct with life. The ant crept forth to her daily toil, the butterfly fluttered and basked in the warm rays of the sun; myriads of insects spread their transparent wings, and revelled in their brief but happy existence. Man walked forth, elated with the scene; and all was brightness and splendour.

"'*You* a miserable man!' said the king of the goblins, in a more contemptuous tone than before. And again the king of the goblins gave his leg a flourish; again it descended on the shoulders of the sexton; and again the attendant goblins imitated the example of their chief.

"Many a time the cloud went and came, and many a lesson it taught to Gabriel Grub, who, although his shoulders smarted with pain from the frequent applications of the goblins' feet thereunto, looked on with an interest that nothing could diminish. He saw that men who worked hard, and earned their scanty bread with lives of labour, were cheerful and happy; and that to the most ignorant, the sweet face of Nature was a never-failing source of cheerfulness and joy. He saw those who had been delicately nurtured, and tenderly brought up, cheerful under privations, and superior to suffering, that would have crushed many of a rougher grain, because they bore within their own bosoms the materials of happiness, contentment, and peace. He saw that women, the tenderest and most fragile of all God's creatures, were the oftenest superior to sorrow, adversity, and distress; and he saw that it was because they bore, in their own hearts, an inexhaustible well-spring of affection and devotion. Above all, he saw that men like himself, who snarled at the mirth and cheerfulness of others, were the foulest weeds on the fair surface of the earth; and setting all the good of the world against the evil, he came to the conclusion that it was a very decent and respectable sort of world after all. No sooner had he formed it, than the cloud which had closed over the last picture, seemed to settle on his senses, and lull him to repose. One by one, the goblins faded from his sight; and, as the last one disappeared, he sank to sleep.

"The day had broken when Gabriel Grub awoke, and found himself lying at full length on the flat gravestone in the churchyard, with the wicker bottle lying empty by his side, and his coat, spade, and lantern, all well whitened by the last night's frost, scattered on the ground. The stone on which he had first seen the goblin seated, stood bolt upright before him, and the grave at which he had worked, the night before, was not far off. At first, he began to doubt the reality of his adventures, but the acute pain in his shoulders when he attempted to rise, assured him that the kicking of the goblins was certainly not ideal. He was staggered again, by observing no traces of footsteps in the snow on which the goblins had played at leap-frog with the gravestones, but he speedily accounted for this circumstance when he remembered that, being spirits, they would leave no visible impression behind them. So, Gabriel Grub got on his feet as well as he could, for the pain in his back; and, brushing the frost off his coat, put it on, and turned his face towards the town.

"But he was an altered man, and he could not bear the thought of returning to a place where his repentance would be scoffed at, and his reformation disbelieved. He hesitated for a few moments; and then turned away to wander where he might, and seek his bread elsewhere.

"The lantern, the spade, and the wicker bottle were found, that day, in the churchyard. There were a great many speculations about the sexton's fate, at first, but it was speedily determined that he had been carried away by the goblins; and there were not wanting some very credible witnesses who had distinctly seen him whisked through the air on the back of a chestnut horse blind of one eye, with the hind-quarters of a lion, and the tail of a bear. At length all this was devoutly believed; and the new sexton used to exhibit to the curious, for a trifling emolument, a good-sized piece of the church weathercock which had been accidentally kicked off by the aforesaid horse in his aerial flight, and picked up by himself in the churchyard, a year or two afterwards.

"Unfortunately, these stories were somewhat disturbed by the unlooked-for reappearance of Gabriel Grub himself, some ten years afterwards, a ragged, contented, rheumatic old man. He told his story to the clergyman, and also to the mayor; and in course of time it began to be received as a matter of history, in which form it has continued down to this very day. The believers in the weathercock tale, having misplaced their confidence once, were not easily prevailed upon to part with it again, so they looked as wise as they could, shrugged their shoulders, touched their foreheads, and murmured something about Gabriel Grub having drunk all the Hollands, and then fallen asleep on the flat tombstone; and they affected to explain what he supposed he had witnessed in the goblin's cavern, by saying that he had seen the world, and grown wiser. But this opinion, which was by no means a popular one at any time, gradually died off; and be the matter how it may, as Gabriel Grub was afflicted with rheumatism to the end of his days, this story has at least one moral, if it teach no better one – and that is, that if a man turn sulky and drink by himself at Christmas time, he may make up his mind to be not a bit the better for it: let the spirits be never so good, or let them be even as many degrees beyond proof, as those which Gabriel Grub saw in the goblin's cavern."

"The Gift of the Magi"
by O Henry

Gift-giving is a very important part of Christmas, and the Nativity story tells us how the Three Wise Men – also known as "the Magi" – brought gifts of gold, frankincense and myrrh to Jesus after his birth.

When writing Christmas lists, it's often pretty easy to decide what you want for yourself, but working out what to get for the special people in your life can be a stressful experience, especially if you don't have much money. The following story is about just this dilemma.

The Gift of the Magi by O Henry is a short story about a young wife trying to work out how to afford the perfect gift for her husband, and it very much embodies the idea that it's "the thought that counts". Its sweet message and ironic twist have made it a beloved part of Christmas tradition.

One dollar and eighty-seven cents. That was all. And sixty cents of it was in pennies. Pennies saved one and two at a time by bulldozing the grocer and the vegetable man and the butcher until one's cheeks burned with the silent imputation of parsimony that such close dealing implied. Three times Della counted it. One dollar and eighty-seven cents. And the next day would be Christmas.

There was clearly nothing to do but flop down on the shabby little couch and howl. So Della did it. Which instigates the moral reflection that life is made up of sobs, sniffles, and smiles, with sniffles predominating.

While the mistress of the home is gradually subsiding from the first stage to the second, take a look at the home. A furnished flat at $8 per week. It did not exactly beggar description, but it certainly had that word on the lookout for the mendicancy squad.

In the vestibule below was a letter-box into which no letter would go, and an electric button from which no mortal finger could coax a ring. Also appertaining thereunto was a card bearing the name "Mr James Dillingham Young."

The "Dillingham" had been flung to the breeze during a former period of prosperity when its possessor was being paid $30 per week. Now, when the income was shrunk to $20, though, they were thinking seriously of contracting to a modest and unassuming D. But whenever Mr James Dillingham Young came home and reached his flat above he was called "Jim" and greatly hugged by Mrs James Dillingham Young, already introduced to you as Della. Which is all very good.

Della finished her cry and attended to her cheeks with the powder rag. She stood by the window and looked out dully at a gray cat walking a gray fence in a gray backyard. Tomorrow would be Christmas Day, and she had only $1.87 with which to buy Jim a present. She had been saving every penny she could for months, with this result. Twenty dollars a week doesn't go far. Expenses had been greater than she had calculated.

They always are. Only $1.87 to buy a present for Jim. Her Jim. Many a happy hour she had spent planning for something nice for him. Something fine and rare and sterling – something just a little bit near to being worthy of the honour of being owned by Jim.

There was a pier glass between the windows of the room. Perhaps you have seen a pier glass in an $8 flat. A very thin and very agile person may, by observing his reflection in a rapid sequence of longitudinal strips, obtain a fairly accurate conception of his looks. Della, being slender, had mastered the art.

Suddenly she whirled from the window and stood before the glass. Her eyes were shining brilliantly, but her face had lost its colour within twenty seconds. Rapidly she pulled down her hair and let it fall to its full length.

Now, there were two possessions of the James Dillingham Youngs in which they both took a mighty pride. One was Jim's gold watch that had been his father's and his grandfather's. The other was Della's hair. Had the queen of Sheba lived in the flat across the airshaft, Della would have let her hair hang out the window some day to dry just to depreciate Her Majesty's jewels and gifts. Had King Solomon been the janitor, with all his treasures piled up in the basement, Jim would have pulled out his watch every time he passed, just to see him pluck at his beard from envy.

So now Della's beautiful hair fell about her rippling and shining like a cascade of brown waters. It reached below her knee and made itself almost a garment for her. And then she did it up again nervously and quickly. Once she faltered for a minute and stood still while a tear or two splashed on the worn red carpet.

On went her old brown jacket; on went her old brown hat. With a whirl of skirts and with the brilliant sparkle still in her eyes, she fluttered out the door and down the stairs to the street.

Where she stopped the sign read: "Mme. Sofronie. Hair Goods of All Kinds." One flight up Della ran, and collected herself, panting. Madame, large, too white, chilly, hardly looked the "Sofronie."

"Will you buy my hair?" asked Della.

"I buy hair," said Madame. "Take yer hat off and let's have a sight at the looks of it."

Down rippled the brown cascade.

"Twenty dollars," said Madame, lifting the mass with a practised hand.

"Give it to me quick," said Della.

Oh, and the next two hours tripped by on rosy wings. Forget the hashed metaphor. She was ransacking the stores for Jim's present.

She found it at last. It surely had been made for Jim and no one else. There was no other like it in any of the stores, and she had turned all of them inside out. It was a platinum fob chain simple and chaste in design, properly proclaiming its value by substance alone and not by meretricious ornamentation – as all good things should do. It was even worthy of The Watch. As soon as she saw it she knew that it must be Jim's. It was like him. Quietness and value – the description applied to both. Twenty-one dollars they took from her for it, and she hurried home with the 87 cents. With that chain on his watch Jim might be properly anxious about the time in any company. Grand as the watch was, he sometimes looked at it on the sly on account of the old leather strap that he used in place of a chain.

When Della reached home her intoxication gave way a little to prudence and reason. She got out her curling irons and lighted the gas and went to work repairing the ravages made by generosity added to love. Which is always a tremendous task, dear friends – a mammoth task.

Within forty minutes her head was covered with tiny,

close-lying curls that made her look wonderfully like a truant schoolboy. She looked at her reflection in the mirror long, carefully, and critically.

"If Jim doesn't kill me," she said to herself, "before he takes a second look at me, he'll say I look like a Coney Island chorus girl. But what could I do – oh! what could I do with a dollar and eighty-seven cents?"

At 7 o'clock the coffee was made and the frying-pan was on the back of the stove hot and ready to cook the chops.

Jim was never late. Della doubled the fob chain in her hand and sat on the corner of the table near the door that he always entered. Then she heard his step on the stair away down on the first flight, and she turned white for just a moment. She had a habit of saying a little silent prayer about the simplest everyday things, and now she whispered: "Please God, make him think I am still pretty."

The door opened and Jim stepped in and closed it. He looked thin and very serious. Poor fellow, he was only twenty-two – and to be burdened with a family! He needed a new overcoat and he was without gloves.

Jim stopped inside the door, as immovable as a setter at the scent of quail. His eyes were fixed upon Della, and there was an expression in them that she could not read, and it terrified her. It was not anger, nor surprise, nor disapproval, nor horror, nor any of the sentiments that she had been prepared for. He simply stared at her fixedly with that peculiar expression on his face.

Della wriggled off the table and went for him.

"Jim, darling," she cried, "don't look at me that way. I had my hair cut off and sold because I couldn't have lived through Christmas without giving you a present. It'll grow out again – you won't mind, will you? I just had to do it. My hair grows awfully fast. Say 'Merry Christmas!' Jim, and let's be happy. You don't know what a nice – what a beautiful, nice gift I've got for you."

"You've cut off your hair?" asked Jim, laboriously, as if he had not arrived at that patent fact yet even after the hardest mental labor.

"Cut it off and sold it," said Della. "Don't you like me just as well, anyhow? I'm me without my hair, ain't I?"

Jim looked about the room curiously.

"You say your hair is gone?" he said, with an air almost of idiocy.

"You needn't look for it," said Della. "It's sold, I tell you – sold and gone, too. It's Christmas Eve, boy. Be good to me, for it went for you. Maybe the hairs of my head were numbered," she went on with sudden serious sweetness, "but nobody could ever count my love for you. Shall I put the chops on, Jim?"

Out of his trance Jim seemed quickly to wake. He enfolded his Della. For ten seconds let us regard with discreet scrutiny some inconsequential object in the other direction. Eight dollars a week or a million a year – what is the difference? A mathematician or a wit would give you the wrong answer. The magi brought valuable gifts, but that was not among them. This dark assertion will be illuminated later on.

Jim drew a package from his overcoat pocket and threw it upon the table.

"Don't make any mistake, Dell," he said, "about me. I don't think there's anything in the way of a haircut or a shave or a shampoo that could make me like my girl any less. But if you'll unwrap that package you may see why you had me going a while at first."

White fingers and nimble tore at the string and paper. And then an ecstatic scream of joy; and then, alas! a quick feminine change to hysterical tears and wails, necessitating the immediate employment of all the comforting powers of the lord of the flat.

For there lay The Combs – the set of combs, side

and back, that Della had worshipped long in a Broadway window. Beautiful combs, pure tortoise shell, with jewelled rims – just the shade to wear in the beautiful vanished hair. They were expensive combs, she knew, and her heart had simply craved and yearned over them without the least hope of possession. And now, they were hers, but the tresses that should have adorned the coveted adornments were gone.

But she hugged them to her bosom, and at length she was able to look up with dim eyes and a smile and say: "My hair grows so fast, Jim!"

And then Della leaped up like a little singed cat and cried, "Oh, oh!"

Jim had not yet seen his beautiful present. She held it out to him eagerly upon her open palm. The dull precious metal seemed to flash with a reflection of her bright and ardent spirit.

"Isn't it a dandy, Jim? I hunted all over town to find it. You'll have to look at the time a hundred times a day now. Give me your watch. I want to see how it looks on it."

Instead of obeying, Jim tumbled down on the couch and put his hands under the back of his head and smiled.

"Dell," said he, "let's put our Christmas presents

away and keep 'em a while. They're too nice to use just at present. I sold the watch to get the money to buy your combs. And now suppose you put the chops on."

The magi, as you know, were wise men – wonderfully wise men – who brought gifts to the Babe in the manger. They invented the art of giving Christmas presents. Being wise, their gifts were no doubt wise ones, possibly bearing the privilege of exchange in case of duplication. And here I have lamely related to you the uneventful chronicle of two foolish children in a flat who most unwisely sacrificed for each other the greatest treasures of their house. But in a last word to the wise of these days let it be said that of all who give gifts these two were the wisest. Of all who give and receive gifts, such as they are wisest. Everywhere they are wisest. They are the magi.

"The Adventure of the Blue Carbuncle"
from *The Adventures of Sherlock Holmes*
by Arthur Conan Doyle

Sherlock Holmes was first created in the novel *A Study in Scarlet* in 1887, and the character quickly became very popular. Between 1891 and 1892, Sir Arthur Conan Doyle wrote a series of short stories featuring the character, which appeared in *The Strand* magazine, including the following story, "The Adventure of the Blue Carbuncle".

It's a classic mystery tale featuring the ingenious clues and startling deductions that have made the detective so beloved, and its Christmastime setting makes it a wonderful treat for the season.

I had called upon my friend Sherlock Holmes upon the second morning after Christmas, with the intention of wishing him the compliments of the season. He was lounging upon the sofa in a purple dressing-gown, a pipe-rack within his reach upon the right, and a pile of crumpled morning papers, evidently newly studied, near at hand. Beside the couch was a wooden chair, and on the angle of the back hung a very seedy and disreputable hard-felt hat, much the worse for wear, and cracked in several places. A lens and a forceps lying upon the seat of the chair suggested that the hat had been suspended in this manner for the purpose of examination.

"You are engaged," said I; "perhaps I interrupt you."

"Not at all. I am glad to have a friend with whom I can discuss my results. The matter is a perfectly trivial one" – he jerked his thumb in the direction of the old hat – "but there are points in connection with it which are not entirely devoid of interest and even of instruction."

I seated myself in his armchair and warmed my hands before his crackling fire, for a sharp frost had set in, and the windows were thick with the ice crystals. "I suppose," I remarked, "that, homely as it looks, this thing has some deadly story linked on to it – that it is the clue which will guide you in the solution of some mystery and the punishment of some crime."

"No, no. No crime," said Sherlock Holmes, laughing. "Only one of those whimsical little incidents which will happen when you have four million human beings all jostling each other within the space of a few square miles. Amid the action and reaction of so dense a swarm of humanity, every possible combination of events may be expected to take place, and many a little problem will be presented which may be striking and bizarre without being criminal. We have already had experience of such."

"So much so," I remarked, "that of the last six cases which I have added to my notes, three have been entirely free of any legal crime."

"Precisely. You allude to my attempt to recover the

Irene Adler papers, to the singular case of Miss Mary Sutherland, and to the adventure of the man with the twisted lip. Well, I have no doubt that this small matter will fall into the same innocent category. You know Peterson, the commissionaire?"

"Yes."

"It is to him that this trophy belongs."

"It is his hat."

"No, no, he found it. Its owner is unknown. I beg that you will look upon it not as a battered billycock but as an intellectual problem. And, first, as to how it came here. It arrived upon Christmas morning, in company with a good fat goose, which is, I have no doubt, roasting at this moment in front of Peterson's fire. The facts are these: about four o'clock on Christmas morning, Peterson, who, as you know, is a very honest fellow, was returning from some small jollification and was making his way homeward down Tottenham Court Road. In front of him he saw, in the gaslight, a tallish man, walking with a slight stagger, and carrying a white goose slung over his shoulder. As he reached the corner of Goodge Street, a row broke out between this stranger and a little knot of roughs. One of the latter knocked off the man's hat, on which he raised his stick to defend himself and, swinging it over his head, smashed the shop window behind him. Peterson had rushed forward to protect the stranger from his assailants; but the man, shocked at having broken the window, and seeing an official-looking person in uniform rushing towards him, dropped his goose, took to his heels, and vanished amid the labyrinth of small streets which lie at the back of Tottenham Court Road. The roughs had also fled at the appearance of Peterson, so that he was left in possession of the field of battle, and also of the spoils of victory in the shape of this battered hat and a most unimpeachable Christmas goose."

"Which surely he restored to their owner?"

"My dear fellow, there lies the problem. It is true that 'For Mrs Henry Baker' was printed upon a small card which was tied to the bird's left leg, and it is also true that the initials 'H. B.' are legible upon the lining of this hat, but as there are some thousands of Bakers, and some hundreds of Henry Bakers in this city of ours, it is not easy to restore lost property to any one of them."

"What, then, did Peterson do?"

"He brought round both hat and goose to me on Christmas morning, knowing that even the smallest problems are of interest to me. The goose we retained until this morning, when there were signs that, in spite of the slight frost, it would be well that it should be eaten without unnecessary delay. Its finder has carried it off, therefore, to fulfil the ultimate destiny of a goose, while I continue to retain the hat of the unknown gentleman who lost his Christmas dinner."

"Did he not advertise?"

"No."

"Then, what clue could you have as to his identity?"

"Only as much as we can deduce."

"From his hat?"

"Precisely."

"But you are joking. What can you gather from this old battered felt?"

"Here is my lens. You know my methods. What can you gather yourself as to the individuality of the man who has worn this article?"

I took the tattered object in my hands and turned it over rather ruefully. It was a very ordinary black hat of the usual round shape, hard and much the worse for wear. The lining had been of red silk, but was a good deal discoloured. There was no maker's name; but, as Holmes had remarked, the initials "H.B." were scrawled upon one side. It was pierced in the brim for a hat-securer, but the elastic was missing. For the rest, it was cracked, exceedingly dusty, and spotted in several places, although there seemed to have been some attempt to hide the discoloured patches by smearing them with ink.

"I can see nothing," said I, handing it back to my friend.

"On the contrary, Watson, you can see everything. You fail, however, to reason from what you see. You are too timid in drawing your inferences."

"Then, pray tell me what it is that you can infer from this hat?"

He picked it up and gazed at it in the peculiar introspective fashion which was characteristic of him. "It is perhaps less suggestive than it might have been," he remarked, "and yet there are a few inferences which are very distinct, and a few others which represent at least a strong balance of probability. That the man was highly intellectual is of course obvious upon the face of it, and also that he was fairly well-to-do within the last three years, although he has now fallen upon evil days. He had foresight, but has less now than formerly, pointing to a moral retrogression, which, when taken with the decline of his fortunes, seems to indicate some evil influence, probably drink, at work upon him. This may account also for the obvious fact that his wife has ceased to love him."

"My dear Holmes!"

"He has, however, retained some degree of self-respect," he continued, disregarding my remonstrance. "He is a man who leads a sedentary life, goes out little, is out of training entirely, is middle-aged, has grizzled hair which he has had cut within the last few days, and which he anoints with lime-cream. These are the more patent facts which are to be deduced from his hat. Also, by the way, that it is extremely improbable that he has gas laid on in his house."

"You are certainly joking, Holmes."

"Not in the least. Is it possible that even now, when I give you these results, you are unable to see how they are attained?"

"I have no doubt that I am very stupid, but I must confess that I am unable to follow you. For example, how did you deduce that this man was intellectual?"

For answer Holmes clapped the hat upon his head. It came right over the forehead and settled upon the bridge of his nose. "It is a question of cubic capacity," said he; "a man with so large a brain must have something in it."

"The decline of his fortunes, then?"

"This hat is three years old. These flat brims curled at the edge came in then. It is a hat of the very best quality. Look at the band of ribbed silk and the excellent lining. If this man could afford to buy so expensive a hat three years ago, and has had no hat since, then he has assuredly gone down in the world."

"Well, that is clear enough, certainly. But how about the foresight and the moral retrogression?"

Sherlock Holmes laughed. "Here is the foresight," said he putting his finger upon the little disc and loop of the hat-securer. "They are never sold upon hats. If this man ordered one, it is a sign of a certain amount of foresight, since he went out of his way to take this precaution against the wind. But since we see that he has broken the elastic and has not troubled to replace it, it is obvious that he has less foresight now than formerly, which is a distinct proof of a weakening nature. On the other hand, he has endeavoured to conceal some of these stains upon the felt by daubing them with ink, which is a sign that he has not entirely lost his self-respect."

"Your reasoning is certainly plausible."

"The further points, that he is middle-aged, that his hair is grizzled, that it has been recently cut, and that he uses lime-cream, are all to be gathered from a close examination of the lower part of the lining. The lens discloses a large number of hair-ends, clean cut by the scissors of the barber. They all appear to be adhesive, and there is a distinct odour of lime-cream. This dust, you will observe, is not the gritty, grey dust of the street but the fluffy brown dust of the house, showing that it has been hung up indoors most of the time, while the marks of moisture upon the inside are proof positive that the wearer perspired very freely, and could therefore, hardly be in the best of training."

"But his wife – you said that she had ceased to love him."

"This hat has not been brushed for weeks. When I see you, my dear Watson, with a week's accumulation of dust upon your hat, and when your wife allows you to go out in such a state, I shall fear that you also have been unfortunate enough to lose your wife's affection."

"But he might be a bachelor."

"Nay, he was bringing home the goose as a peace-offering to his wife. Remember the card upon the bird's leg."

"You have an answer to everything. But how on earth do you deduce that the gas is not laid on in his house?"

"One tallow stain, or even two, might come by chance; but when I see no less than five, I think that there can be little doubt that the individual must be brought into frequent contact with burning tallow – walks upstairs at night probably with his hat in one hand and a guttering candle in the other. Anyhow, he never got tallow-stains from a gas-jet. Are you satisfied?"

"Well, it is very ingenious," said I, laughing; "but since, as you said just now, there has been no crime committed, and no harm done save the loss of a goose, all this seems to be rather a waste of energy."

Sherlock Holmes had opened his mouth to reply, when the door flew open, and Peterson, the commissionaire, rushed into the apartment with flushed cheeks and the face of a man who is dazed with astonishment.

"The goose, Mr Holmes! The goose, sir!" he gasped.

"Eh? What of it, then? Has it returned to life and flapped off through the kitchen window?" Holmes twisted himself round upon the sofa to get a fairer view of the man's excited face.

"See here, sir! See what my wife found in its crop!" He held out his hand and displayed upon the centre of the palm a brilliantly scintillating blue stone, rather smaller than a bean in size, but of such purity and radiance that it twinkled like an electric point in the dark hollow of his hand.

Sherlock Holmes sat up with a whistle. "By Jove, Peterson!" said he, "this is treasure trove indeed. I suppose you know what you have got?"

"A diamond, sir? A precious stone. It cuts into glass as though it were putty."

"It's more than a precious stone. It is *the* precious stone."

"Not the Countess of Morcar's blue carbuncle!" I ejaculated.

"Precisely so. I ought to know its size and shape, seeing that I have read the advertisement about it in *The Times* every day lately. It is absolutely unique, and its value can only be conjectured, but the reward offered of a thousand pounds is certainly not within a twentieth part of the market price."

"A thousand pounds! Great Lord of mercy!" The commissionaire plumped down into a chair and stared from one to the other of us.

"That is the reward, and I have reason to know that there are sentimental considerations in the background which would induce the Countess to part with half her fortune if she could but recover the gem."

"It was lost, if I remember aright, at the Hotel Cosmopolitan," I remarked.

"Precisely so, on the twenty-second of December, just five days ago. John Horner, a plumber, was accused of having abstracted it from the lady's jewel-case. The evidence against him was so strong that the case has been referred to the Assizes. I have some account of the matter here, I believe." He rummaged amid his newspapers, glancing over the dates, until at last he smoothed one out, doubled it over, and read the following paragraph:

"Hotel Cosmopolitan Jewel Robbery. John Horner, 26, plumber, was brought up upon the charge of having upon the 22nd inst., abstracted from the jewel-case of the Countess of Morcar the valuable gem known as the blue carbuncle. James Ryder, upper-attendant at the hotel, gave his evidence to the effect that he had shown Horner up to the dressing-room of the Countess of Morcar upon the day of the robbery in order that he might solder the second bar of the grate, which was loose. He had remained with Horner some little time, but had finally been called away. On returning, he found that Horner had disappeared, that the bureau had been forced open, and that the small morocco casket in which, as it afterwards transpired, the Countess was accustomed to keep her jewel, was lying empty upon the dressing-table. Ryder instantly gave the alarm, and Horner was arrested the same evening; but the stone could not be found either upon his person or in his rooms. Catherine Cusack, maid to the Countess, deposed to having heard Ryder's cry of dismay on discovering the robbery, and to having rushed into the room, where she found matters as described by the last witness. Inspector Bradstreet, B division, gave evidence as to the arrest of Horner, who struggled frantically, and protested his innocence in the strongest terms. Evidence of a previous conviction for robbery having been given against the prisoner, the magistrate refused to deal summarily with the offence, but referred it to the Assizes. Horner, who had shown signs of intense emotion during the proceedings, fainted away at the conclusion and was carried out of court."

"Hum! So much for the police-court," said Holmes thoughtfully, tossing aside the paper. "The question for us now to solve is the sequence of events leading from a rifled jewel-case at one end to the crop of a goose in Tottenham Court Road at the other. You see, Watson, our little deductions have suddenly assumed a much more important and less innocent aspect. Here is the stone; the stone came from the goose, and the goose came from Mr Henry Baker, the gentleman with the bad hat and all the other characteristics with which I have bored you. So now we must set ourselves very seriously to finding this gentleman and ascertaining what part he has played in this little mystery. To do this, we must try the simplest means first, and these lie undoubtedly in an advertisement in all the evening papers. If this fail, I shall have recourse to other methods."

"What will you say?"

"Give me a pencil and that slip of paper. Now, then: 'Found at the corner of Goodge Street, a goose and a black felt hat. Mr Henry Baker can have the same by applying at 6:30 this evening at 221B, Baker Street.' That is clear and concise."

"Very. But will he see it?"

"Well, he is sure to keep an eye on the papers, since, to a poor man, the loss was a heavy one. He was clearly so scared by his mischance in breaking the window and by the approach of Peterson that he thought of nothing but flight, but since then he must have bitterly regretted the impulse which caused him to drop his bird. Then, again, the introduction of his name will cause him to see it, for everyone who knows him will direct his attention to it. Here you are, Peterson, run down to the advertising agency and have this put in the evening papers."

"In which, sir?"

"Oh, in the *Globe, Star, Pall Mall, St. James's, Evening News, Standard, Echo*, and any others that occur to you."

"Very well, sir. And this stone?"

"Ah, yes, I shall keep the stone. Thank you. And, I say, Peterson, just buy a goose on your way back and leave it here with me, for we must have one to give to this gentleman in place of the one which your family is now devouring."

When the commissionaire had gone, Holmes took up the stone and held it against the light. "It's a bonny thing," said he. "Just see how it glints and sparkles. Of course it is a nucleus and focus of crime. Every good stone is. They are the devil's pet baits. In the larger and older jewels every facet may stand for a bloody deed. This stone is not yet twenty years old. It was found in the banks of the Amoy River in southern China and is remarkable in having every characteristic of the carbuncle, save that it is blue in shade instead of ruby red. In spite of its youth, it has already a sinister history. There have been two murders, a vitriol-throwing, a suicide, and several robberies brought about for the sake of this forty-grain weight of crystallised charcoal. Who would think that so pretty a toy would be a purveyor to the gallows and the prison? I'll lock it up in my strong box now and drop a line to the Countess to say that we have it."

"Do you think that this man Horner is innocent?"

"I cannot tell."

"Well, then, do you imagine that this other one, Henry Baker, had anything to do with the matter?"

"It is, I think, much more likely that Henry Baker is an absolutely innocent man, who had no idea that the bird which he was carrying was of considerably more value than if it were made of solid gold. That, however, I shall determine by a very simple test if we have an answer to our advertisement."

"And you can do nothing until then?"

"Nothing."

"In that case I shall continue my professional round. But I shall come back in the evening at the hour you have mentioned, for I should like to see the solution of so tangled a business."

"Very glad to see you. I dine at seven. There is a woodcock, I believe. By the way, in view of recent occurrences, perhaps I ought to ask Mrs Hudson to examine its crop."

I had been delayed at a case, and it was a little after half-past six when I found myself in Baker Street once more. As I approached the house I saw a tall man in a Scotch bonnet with a coat which was buttoned up to his chin waiting outside in the bright semicircle which was thrown from the fanlight. Just as I arrived the door was opened, and we were shown up together to Holmes' room.

"Mr Henry Baker, I believe," said he, rising from his armchair and greeting his visitor with the easy air of geniality which he could so readily assume. "Pray take this chair by the fire, Mr Baker. It is a cold night, and I observe that your circulation is more adapted for summer than for winter. Ah, Watson, you have just come at the right time. Is that your hat, Mr Baker?"

"Yes, sir, that is undoubtedly my hat."

He was a large man with rounded shoulders, a massive head, and a broad, intelligent face, sloping down to a pointed beard of grizzled brown. A touch of red in nose and cheeks, with a slight tremor of his extended hand, recalled Holmes' surmise as to his habits. His rusty black frock-coat was buttoned right up in front, with the collar turned up, and his lank wrists protruded from his sleeves without a sign of cuff or shirt. He spoke in a slow staccato fashion, choosing his words with care, and gave the impression generally of a man of learning and letters who had had ill-usage at the hands of fortune.

"We have retained these things for some days," said Holmes, "because we expected to see an advertisement from you giving your address. I am at a loss to know now why you did not advertise."

Our visitor gave a rather shamefaced laugh. "Shillings have not been so plentiful with me as they once were," he remarked. "I had no doubt that the gang of roughs who assaulted me had carried off both my hat and the bird. I did not care to spend more money in a hopeless attempt at recovering them."

"Very naturally. By the way, about the bird, we were compelled to eat it."

"To eat it!" Our visitor half rose from his chair in his excitement.

"Yes, it would have been of no use to anyone had

we not done so. But I presume that this other goose upon the sideboard, which is about the same weight and perfectly fresh, will answer your purpose equally well?"

"Oh, certainly, certainly," answered Mr Baker with a sigh of relief.

"Of course, we still have the feathers, legs, crop, and so on of your own bird, so if you wish—"

The man burst into a hearty laugh. "They might be useful to me as relics of my adventure," said he, "but beyond that I can hardly see what use the *disjecta membra* of my late acquaintance are going to be to me. No, sir, I think that, with your permission, I will confine my attentions to the excellent bird which I perceive upon the sideboard."

Sherlock Holmes glanced sharply across at me with a slight shrug of his shoulders.

"There is your hat, then, and there your bird," said he. "By the way, would it bore you to tell me where you got the other one from? I am somewhat of a fowl fancier, and I have seldom seen a better-grown goose."

"Certainly, sir," said Baker, who had risen and tucked his newly gained property under his arm. "There are a few of us who frequent the Alpha Inn, near the Museum – we are to be found in the Museum itself during the day, you understand. This year our good host, Windigate by name, instituted a goose club, by which, on consideration of some few pence every week, we were each to receive a bird at Christmas. My pence were duly paid, and the rest is familiar to you. I am much indebted to you, sir, for a Scotch bonnet is fitted neither to my years nor my gravity." With a comical pomposity of manner he bowed solemnly to both of us and strode off upon his way.

"So much for Mr Henry Baker," said Holmes when he had closed the door behind him. "It is quite certain that he knows nothing whatever about the matter. Are you hungry, Watson?"

"Not particularly."

"Then I suggest that we turn our dinner into a supper and follow up this clue while it is still hot."

"By all means."

It was a bitter night, so we drew on our ulsters and wrapped cravats about our throats. Outside, the stars were shining coldly in a cloudless sky, and the breath of the passers-by blew out into smoke like so many pistol shots. Our footfalls rang out crisply and loudly as we swung through the doctors' quarter, Wimpole Street, Harley Street, and so through Wigmore Street into Oxford Street. In a quarter of an hour we were in Bloomsbury at the Alpha Inn, which is a small public-house at the corner of one of the streets which runs down into Holborn. Holmes pushed open the door of the private bar and ordered two glasses of beer from the ruddy-faced, white-aproned landlord.

"Your beer should be excellent if it is as good as your geese," said he.

"My geese!" The man seemed surprised.

"Yes. I was speaking only half an hour ago to Mr Henry Baker, who was a member of your goose club."

"Ah! yes, I see. But you see, sir, them's not *our* geese."

"Indeed! Whose, then?"

"Well, I got the two dozen from a salesman in Covent Garden."

"Indeed? I know some of them. Which was it?"

"Breckinridge is his name."

"Ah! I don't know him. Well, here's your good health landlord, and prosperity to your house. Good-night."

"Now for Mr Breckinridge," he continued, buttoning up his coat as we came out into the frosty air. "Remember, Watson that though we have so homely a thing as a goose at one end of this chain, we have at the other a man who will certainly get seven years' penal servitude unless we can establish his innocence. It is possible that our inquiry may but confirm his guilt; but, in any case, we have a line of investigation which has been missed by the police, and which a singular chance has placed in our hands. Let us follow it out to the bitter end. Faces to the south, then, and quick march!"

We passed across Holborn, down Endell Street, and so through a zigzag of slums to Covent Garden Market. One of the largest stalls bore the name of Breckinridge upon it, and the proprietor a horsey-looking man, with a sharp face and trim side-whiskers was helping a boy to put up the shutters.

"Good-evening. It's a cold night," said Holmes.

The salesman nodded and shot a questioning glance at my companion.

"Sold out of geese, I see," continued Holmes, pointing at the bare slabs of marble.

"Let you have five hundred tomorrow morning."

"That's no good."

"Well, there are some on the stall with the gas-flare."

"Ah, but I was recommended to you."

"Who by?"

"The landlord of the Alpha."

"Oh, yes; I sent him a couple of dozen."

"Fine birds they were, too. Now where did you get them from?"

To my surprise the question provoked a burst of anger from the salesman.

"Now, then, mister," said he, with his head cocked and his arms akimbo, "what are you driving at? Let's have it straight, now."

"It is straight enough. I should like to know who sold you the geese which you supplied to the Alpha."

"Well then, I shan't tell you. So now!"

"Oh, it is a matter of no importance; but I don't know why you should be so warm over such a trifle."

"Warm! You'd be as warm, maybe, if you were as pestered as I am. When I pay good money for a good article there should be an end of the business; but it's 'Where are the geese?' and 'Who did you sell the geese to?' and 'What will you take for the geese?' One would think they were the only geese in the world, to hear the fuss that is made over them."

"Well, I have no connection with any other people who have been making inquiries," said Holmes carelessly. "If you won't tell us the bet is off, that is all. But I'm always ready to back my opinion on a matter of fowls, and I have a fiver on it that the bird I ate is country bred."

"Well, then, you've lost your fiver, for it's town bred," snapped the salesman.

"It's nothing of the kind."

"I say it is."

"I don't believe it."

"D'you think you know more about fowls than I, who have handled them ever since I was a nipper? I tell you, all those birds that went to the Alpha were town bred."

"You'll never persuade me to believe that."

"Will you bet, then?"

"It's merely taking your money, for I know that I am right. But I'll have a sovereign on with you, just to teach you not to be obstinate."

The salesman chuckled grimly. "Bring me the books, Bill," said he.

The small boy brought round a small thin volume and a great greasy-backed one, laying them out together beneath the hanging lamp.

"Now then, Mr Cocksure," said the salesman, "I thought that I was out of geese, but before I finish you'll find that there is still one left in my shop. You see this little book?"

"Well?"

"That's the list of the folk from whom I buy. D'you see?

Well, then, here on this page are the country folk, and the numbers after their names are where their accounts are in the big ledger. Now, then! You see this other page in red ink? Well, that is a list of my town suppliers. Now, look at that third name. Just read it out to me."

"Mrs Oakshott, 117, Brixton Road – 249," read Holmes.

"Quite so. Now turn that up in the ledger."

Holmes turned to the page indicated. "Here you are, 'Mrs Oakshott, 117, Brixton Road, egg and poultry supplier.'"

"Now, then, what's the last entry?"

"'December 22. Twenty-four geese at 7s. 6d.'"

"Quite so. There you are. And underneath?"

"'Sold to Mr Windigate of the Alpha, at 12s.'"

"What have you to say now?"

Sherlock Holmes looked deeply chagrined. He drew a sovereign from his pocket and threw it down upon the slab, turning away with the air of a man whose disgust is too deep for words. A few yards off he stopped under a lamp-post and laughed in the hearty, noiseless fashion which was peculiar to him.

"When you see a man with whiskers of that cut and the 'Pink 'un' protruding out of his pocket, you can always draw him by a bet," said he. "I daresay that if I had put £100 down in front of him, that man would not have given me such complete information as was drawn from him by the idea that he was doing me on a wager. Well, Watson, we are, I fancy, nearing the end of our quest, and the only point which remains to be determined is whether we should go on to this Mrs Oakshott tonight, or whether we should reserve it for tomorrow. It is clear from what that surly fellow said that there are others besides ourselves who are anxious about the matter, and I should—"

His remarks were suddenly cut short by a loud hubbub which broke out from the stall which we had just left. Turning round we saw a little rat-faced fellow standing in the centre of the circle of yellow light which was thrown by the swinging lamp, while Breckinridge, the salesman, framed in the door of his stall, was shaking his fists fiercely at the cringing figure.

"I've had enough of you and your geese," he shouted. "I wish you were all at the devil together. If you come pestering me any more with your silly talk I'll set the dog at you. You bring Mrs Oakshott here and I'll answer her, but what have you to do with it? Did I buy the geese off you?"

"No; but one of them was mine all the same," whined the little man.

"Well, then, ask Mrs Oakshott for it."

"She told me to ask you."

"Well, you can ask the King of Proosia, for all I care. I've had enough of it. Get out of this!" He rushed fiercely forward, and the inquirer flitted away into the darkness.

"Ha! this may save us a visit to Brixton Road," whispered Holmes. "Come with me, and we will see what is to be made of this fellow." Striding through the scattered knots of people who lounged round the flaring stalls, my companion speedily overtook the little man and touched him upon the shoulder. He sprang round, and I could see in the gas-light that every vestige of colour had been driven from his face.

"Who are you, then? What do you want?" he asked in a quavering voice.

"You will excuse me," said Holmes blandly, "but I could not help overhearing the questions which you put to the salesman just now. I think that I could be of assistance to you."

"You? Who are you? How could you know anything of the matter?"

"My name is Sherlock Holmes. It is my business to know what other people don't know."

"But you can know nothing of this?"

"Excuse me, I know everything of it. You are endeavouring to trace some geese which were sold by Mrs Oakshott, of Brixton Road, to a salesman named Breckinridge, by him in turn to Mr Windigate, of the Alpha, and by him to his club, of which Mr Henry Baker is a member."

"Oh, sir, you are the very man whom I have longed to meet," cried the little fellow with outstretched hands and quivering fingers. "I can hardly explain to you how interested I am in this matter."

Sherlock Holmes hailed a four-wheeler which was passing. "In that case we had better discuss it in a cosy room rather than in this wind-swept market-place," said he. "But pray tell me, before we go farther, who it is that I have the pleasure of assisting."

The man hesitated for an instant. "My name is John Robinson," he answered with a sidelong glance.

"No, no; the real name," said Holmes sweetly. "It is always awkward doing business with an alias."

A flush sprang to the white cheeks of the stranger. "Well then," said he, "my real name is James Ryder."

"Precisely so. Head attendant at the Hotel Cosmopolitan. Pray step into the cab, and I shall soon be able to tell you everything which you would wish to know."

The little man stood glancing from one to the other of us with half-frightened, half-hopeful eyes, as one who is not sure whether he is on the verge of a windfall or of a catastrophe. Then he stepped into the cab, and in half an hour we were back in the sitting-room at Baker Street. Nothing had been said during our drive, but the high, thin breathing of our new companion, and the claspings and unclaspings of his hands, spoke of the nervous tension within him.

"Here we are!" said Holmes cheerily as we filed into the room. "The fire looks very seasonable in this weather. You look cold, Mr Ryder. Pray take the basket-chair. I will just put on my slippers before we settle this little matter of yours. Now, then! You want to know what became of those geese?"

"Yes, sir."

"Or rather, I fancy, of that goose. It was one bird, I imagine in which you were interested – white, with a black bar across the tail."

Ryder quivered with emotion. "Oh, sir," he cried, "can you tell me where it went to?"

"It came here."

"Here?"

"Yes, and a most remarkable bird it proved. I don't wonder that you should take an interest in it. It laid an egg after it was dead – the bonniest, brightest little blue egg that ever was seen. I have it here in my museum."

Our visitor staggered to his feet and clutched the mantelpiece with his right hand. Holmes unlocked his strong-box and held up the blue carbuncle, which shone out like a star, with a cold, brilliant, many-pointed radiance. Ryder stood glaring with a drawn face, uncertain whether to claim or to disown it.

"The game's up, Ryder," said Holmes quietly. "Hold up, man, or you'll be into the fire! Give him an arm back into his chair, Watson. He's not got blood enough to go in for felony with impunity. Give him a dash of brandy. So! Now he looks a little more human. What a shrimp it is, to be sure!"

For a moment he had staggered and nearly fallen, but the brandy brought a tinge of colour into his cheeks, and he sat staring with frightened eyes at his accuser.

"I have almost every link in my hands, and all the proofs which I could possibly need, so there is little which you need tell me. Still, that little may as well be cleared up to make the case complete. You had heard, Ryder, of this blue stone of the Countess of Morcar's?"

"It was Catherine Cusack who told me of it," said he in a crackling voice.

"I see – her ladyship's waiting-maid. Well, the temptation of sudden wealth so easily acquired was too much for you, as it has been for better men before you; but you were not very scrupulous in the means you used. It seems to me, Ryder, that there is the making of a very pretty villain in you. You knew that this man Horner, the plumber, had been concerned in some such matter before, and that suspicion would rest the more readily upon him. What did you do, then? You made some small job in my lady's room – you and your confederate Cusack – and you managed that he should be the man sent for. Then, when he had left, you rifled the jewel-case, raised the alarm, and had this unfortunate man arrested. You then—"

Ryder threw himself down suddenly upon the rug and clutched at my companion's knees. "For God's sake, have mercy!" he shrieked. "Think of my father! Of my mother! It would break their hearts. I never went wrong before! I never will again. I swear it. I'll swear it on a Bible. Oh, don't bring it into court! For Christ's sake, don't!"

"Get back into your chair!" said Holmes sternly. "It is very well to cringe and crawl now, but you thought little enough of this poor Horner in the dock for a crime of which he knew nothing."

"I will fly, Mr Holmes. I will leave the country, sir. Then the charge against him will break down."

"Hum! We will talk about that. And now let us hear a true account of the next act. How came the stone into the goose, and how came the goose into the open market? Tell us the truth, for there lies your only hope of safety."

Ryder passed his tongue over his parched lips. "I will tell you it just as it happened, sir," said he. "When Horner had been arrested, it seemed to me that it would be best for me to get away with the stone at once, for I did not know at what moment the police might not take it into their heads to search me and my room. There was no place about the hotel where it would be safe. I went out, as if on some commission, and I made for my sister's house. She had married a man named Oakshott, and lived in Brixton Road, where she fattened fowls for the market. All the way there every man I met seemed to me to be a policeman or a detective; and, for all that it was a cold night, the sweat was pouring down my face before I came to the Brixton Road. My sister asked me what was the matter, and why I was so pale; but I told her that I had been upset by the jewel robbery at the hotel. Then I went into the back yard and smoked a pipe and wondered what it would be best to do.

"I had a friend once called Maudsley, who went to the bad, and has just been serving his time in Pentonville. One day he had met me, and fell into talk about the ways of thieves, and how they could get rid of what they stole. I knew that he would be true to me, for I knew one or two things about him; so I made up my mind to go right on to Kilburn, where he lived, and take him into my confidence. He would show me how to turn the stone into money. But how to get to him in safety? I thought of the agonies I had gone through in coming from the hotel. I might at any moment be seized and searched, and there would be the stone in my waistcoat pocket. I was leaning against the wall at the time and looking at the geese which were waddling about round my feet, and suddenly an idea came into my head which showed me how I could beat the best detective that ever lived.

"My sister had told me some weeks before that I might have the pick of her geese for a Christmas present, and I knew that she was always as good as her word. I would take my goose now, and in it I would carry my stone to Kilburn. There was a little shed in the yard, and behind this I drove one of the birds – a fine big one, white, with a barred tail. I caught it, and prying its bill open, I thrust the stone down its throat as far as my finger could reach. The bird gave a gulp, and I felt the stone pass along its gullet and down into its crop. But the creature flapped and struggled, and out came my sister to know what was the matter. As I turned to speak to her the brute broke loose and fluttered off among the others.

"'Whatever were you doing with that bird, Jem?' says she.

"'Well,' said I, 'you said you'd give me one for Christmas, and I was feeling which was the fattest.'

"'Oh,' says she, 'we've set yours aside for you – Jem's bird, we call it. It's the big white one over yonder. There's twenty-six of them, which makes one for you, and one for us, and two dozen for the market.'

"'Thank you, Maggie,' says I; 'but if it is all the same to you, I'd rather have that one I was handling just now.'

"'The other is a good three pound heavier,' said she, 'and we fattened it expressly for you.'

"'Never mind. I'll have the other, and I'll take it now,' said I.

"'Oh, just as you like,' said she, a little huffed. 'Which is it you want, then?'

"'That white one with the barred tail, right in the middle of the flock.'

"'Oh, very well. Kill it and take it with you.'

"Well, I did what she said, Mr Holmes, and I carried the bird all the way to Kilburn. I told my pal what I had done, for he was a man that it was easy to tell a thing like that to. He laughed until he choked, and we got a knife and opened the goose. My heart turned to water, for there was no sign of the stone, and I knew that some terrible mistake had occurred. I left the bird, rushed back to my sister's, and hurried into the back yard. There was not a bird to be seen there.

"'Where are they all, Maggie?' I cried.

"'Gone to the dealer's, Jem.'

"'Which dealer's?'

"'Breckinridge, of Covent Garden.'

"'But was there another with a barred tail?' I asked, 'the same as the one I chose?'

"'Yes, Jem; there were two barred-tailed ones, and I could never tell them apart.'

"Well, then, of course I saw it all, and I ran off as hard as my feet would carry me to this man Breckinridge; but he had sold the lot at once, and not one word would he tell me as to where they had gone. You heard him yourselves tonight. Well, he has always answered me like that. My sister thinks that I am going mad. Sometimes I think that I am myself. And now – and now I am myself a branded thief, without ever having touched the wealth for which I sold my character. God help me! God help me!" He burst into convulsive sobbing, with his face buried in his hands.

There was a long silence, broken only by his heavy breathing and by the measured tapping of Sherlock Holmes' finger-tips upon the edge of the table. Then my friend rose and threw open the door.

"Get out!" said he.

"What, sir! Oh, Heaven bless you!"

"No more words. Get out!"

And no more words were needed. There was a rush, a clatter upon the stairs, the bang of a door, and the crisp rattle of running footfalls from the street.

"After all, Watson," said Holmes, reaching up his hand for his clay pipe, "I am not retained by the police to supply their deficiencies. If Horner were in danger it would be another thing; but this fellow will not appear against him, and the case must collapse. I suppose that I am commuting a felony, but it is just possible that I am saving a soul. This fellow will not go wrong again; he is too terribly frightened. Send him to gaol now, and you make him a gaol-bird for life. Besides, it is the season of forgiveness. Chance has put in our way a most singular and whimsical problem, and its solution is its own reward. If you will have the goodness to touch the bell, Doctor, we will begin another investigation, in which, also a bird will be the chief feature."

"Dulce Domum"
from *The Wind in the Willows*
by Kenneth Grahame

For many there is nothing more wonderful about Christmastime than the opportunity to visit home, and people travel from far and wide to spend the season with their families. Few pieces of literature capture this intense yearning for home like the "Dulce Domum" chapter of Kenneth Grahame's *The Wind in the Willows*. In fact, the chapter title literally means "sweet home".

At the beginning of the book, Mole is spring-cleaning his hole when he suddenly feels an intense dissatisfaction with his boring old life, and so he sets out in search of excitement. He soon finds a river and meets Rat, and the two become firm friends, having lots of exciting adventures together.

But as the following chapter begins in the middle of a snowy December, Mole is seized just as suddenly with a need to return to the home he left. What follows is a wonderfully festive chapter as Mole invites Rat to spend the evening with him, and must decide whether he prefers the excitement of his new life or the comforting familiarity of his old.

The sheep ran huddling together against the hurdles, blowing out thin nostrils and stamping with delicate forefeet, their heads thrown back and a light steam rising from the crowded sheep-pen into the frosty air, as the two animals hastened by in high spirits, with much chatter and laughter. They were returning across country after a long day's outing with Otter, hunting and exploring on the wide uplands where certain streams tributary to their own River had their first small beginnings; and the shades of the short winter day were closing in on them, and they had still some distance to go. Plodding at random across the plough, they had heard the sheep and had made for them; and now, leading from the sheep-pen, they found a beaten track that made walking a lighter business, and responded, moreover, to that small inquiring something which all animals carry inside them, saying unmistakably, "Yes, quite right; *this* leads home!"

"It looks as if we were coming to a village," said the Mole somewhat dubiously, slackening his pace, as the track, that had in time become a path and then had developed into a lane, now handed them over to the charge of a well-metalled road. The animals did not hold with villages, and their own highways, thickly frequented as they were, took an independent course, regardless of church, post office, or public-house.

"Oh, never mind!" said the Rat. "At this season of the year they're all safe indoors by this time, sitting round the fire; men, women, and children, dogs and cats and all. We shall slip through all right, without any bother or unpleasantness, and we can have a look at them through their windows if you like, and see what they're doing."

The rapid nightfall of mid-December had quite beset the little village as they approached it on soft feet over a first thin fall of powdery snow. Little was visible but squares of a dusky orange-red on either side of the street, where the firelight or lamplight of each cottage overflowed through the casements into the dark world without. Most of the low latticed windows were innocent of blinds, and to the lookers-in from outside, the inmates, gathered round the tea-table, absorbed in handiwork, or talking with laughter and gesture, had each that happy grace which is the last thing the skilled actor shall capture – the natural grace which goes with perfect unconsciousness of observation. Moving at will from one theatre to another, the two spectators, so far from home themselves, had something of wistfulness in their eyes as they watched a cat being stroked, a sleepy child picked up and huddled off to bed, or a tired man stretch and knock out his pipe on the end of a smouldering log.

But it was from one little window, with its blind drawn down, a mere blank transparency on the night, that the sense of home and the little curtained world within walls – the larger stressful world of outside Nature shut out and forgotten – most pulsated. Close against the white blind hung a birdcage, clearly silhouetted, every wire, perch, and appurtenance distinct and recognizable, even to yesterday's dull-edged lump of sugar. On the middle perch the fluffy occupant, head tucked well into feathers, seemed so near to them as to be easily stroked, had they tried; even the delicate tips of his plumped-out plumage pencilled plainly on the illuminated screen. As they looked, the sleepy little fellow stirred uneasily, woke, shook himself, and raised his head. They could see the gape of his tiny beak as he yawned in a bored sort of way, looked round, and then settled his head into his back again, while the ruffled feathers gradually subsided into perfect stillness. Then a gust of bitter wind took them in the back of the neck, a small sting of frozen sleet on the skin woke them as from a dream, and they knew their toes to be cold and their legs tired, and their own home distant a weary way.

Once beyond the village, where the cottages ceased abruptly, on either side of the road they could smell through the darkness the friendly fields again; and they braced themselves for the last long stretch, the home stretch, the stretch that we know is bound to end, some time, in the rattle of the door-latch, the sudden firelight, and the sight of familiar things greeting us as long-absent travellers from far over-sea. They plodded along steadily and silently, each of them thinking his own thoughts. The Mole's ran a good deal on supper, as it was pitch-dark, and it was all a strange country for him as far as he knew, and he was following obediently in the wake of the Rat, leaving the guidance entirely to him. As for the Rat, he was walking a little way ahead, as his habit was, his shoulders humped, his eyes fixed on the straight grey road in front of him; so he did not notice poor Mole when suddenly the summons reached him, and took him like an electric shock.

We others, who have long lost the more subtle of the physical senses, have not even proper terms to express an animal's inter-communications with his surroundings, living or otherwise, and have only the word "smell," for instance, to include the whole range of delicate thrills which murmur in the nose of the animal night and day, summoning, warning, inciting, repelling. It was one of these mysterious fairy calls from out the void that suddenly reached Mole in the darkness, making him tingle through and through with its very familiar appeal, even while yet he could not clearly remember what it was. He stopped dead in his tracks, his nose searching hither and thither in its efforts to recapture the fine filament, the telegraphic current, that had so strongly moved him. A moment, and he had caught it again; and with it this time came recollection in fullest flood.

Home! That was what they meant, those caressing appeals, those soft touches wafted through the air, those invisible little hands pulling and tugging, all one way! Why, it must be quite close by him at that moment, his old home that he had hurriedly forsaken and never sought again, that day when he first found the river! And now it was sending out its scouts and its messengers to capture him and bring him in. Since his escape on that bright morning he had hardly given it a thought, so absorbed had he been in his new life, in all its pleasures, its surprises, its fresh and captivating experiences. Now, with a rush of old memories, how clearly it stood up before him, in the darkness! Shabby indeed, and small and poorly furnished, and yet his, the home he had made for himself, the home he had been so happy to get back to after his day's work. And the home had been happy with him, too, evidently, and was missing him, and wanted him back, and was telling him so, through his nose, sorrowfully, reproachfully, but with no bitterness or anger; only with plaintive reminder that it was there, and wanted him.

The call was clear, the summons was plain. He must obey it instantly, and go. "Ratty!" he called, full of joyful excitement, "hold on! Come back! I want you, quick!"

"Oh, *come* along, Mole, do!" replied the Rat cheerfully, still plodding along.

"*Please* stop, Ratty!" pleaded the poor Mole, in anguish of heart. "You don't understand! It's my home, my old home! I've just come across the smell of it, and it's close by here, really quite close. And I must go to it, I must, I must! Oh, come back, Ratty! Please, please come back!"

The Rat was by this time very far ahead, too far to hear clearly what the Mole was calling, too far to catch the sharp note of painful appeal in his voice. And he was much taken up with the weather, for he too could smell something – something suspiciously like approaching snow.

"Mole, we mustn't stop now, really!" he called back. "We'll come for it tomorrow, whatever it is you've found. But I daren't stop now – it's late, and the snow's coming on again, and I'm not sure of the way! And I want your nose, Mole, so come on quick, there's a good fellow!" And the Rat pressed forward on his way without waiting for an answer.

Poor Mole stood alone in the road, his heart torn asunder, and a big sob gathering, gathering, somewhere low down inside him, to leap up to the surface presently, he knew, in passionate escape. But even under such a test as this his loyalty to his friend stood firm. Never for a moment did he dream of abandoning him. Meanwhile, the wafts from his old home pleaded, whispered, conjured, and finally claimed him imperiously. He dared not tarry longer within their magic circle. With a wrench that tore his very heartstrings he set his face down the road and followed submissively in the track of the Rat, while faint, thin little smells, still dogging his retreating nose, reproached him for his new friendship and his callous forgetfulness.

With an effort he caught up to the unsuspecting Rat, who began chattering cheerfully about what they would do when they got back, and how jolly a fire of logs in the parlour would be, and what a supper he meant to eat; never noticing his companion's silence and distressful state of mind. At last, however, when they had gone some considerable way further, and were passing some tree-stumps at the edge of a copse that bordered the road, he stopped and said kindly, "Look here, Mole old chap, you seem dead tired. No talk left in you, and your feet dragging like lead. We'll sit down here for a minute and rest. The snow has held off so far, and the best part of our journey is over."

The Mole subsided forlornly on a tree-stump and tried to control himself, for he felt it surely coming. The sob he had fought with so long refused to be beaten. Up and up, it forced its way to the air, and then another, and another, and others thick and fast; till poor Mole at last gave up the struggle, and cried freely and helplessly and openly, now that he knew it was all over and he had lost what he could hardly be said to have found.

The Rat, astonished and dismayed at the violence of Mole's paroxysm of grief, did not dare to speak for a while. At last he said, very quietly and sympathetically, "What is it, old fellow? Whatever can be the matter? Tell us your trouble, and let me see what I can do."

Poor Mole found it difficult to get any words out between the upheavals of his chest that followed one upon another so quickly and held back speech and choked it as it came. "I know it's a – shabby, dingy little place," he sobbed forth at last, brokenly: "not like – your cosy quarters – or Toad's beautiful hall – or Badger's great house – but it was my own little home – and I was fond of it – and I went away and forgot all about it – and then I smelt it suddenly – on the road, when I called and you wouldn't listen, Rat – and everything came back to me with a rush – and I *wanted* it! – O dear, O dear! – and when you *wouldn't* turn back, Ratty – and I had to leave it, though I was smelling it all the time – I thought my heart would break. – We might have just gone and had one look at it, Ratty – only one look – it was close by – but you wouldn't turn back, Ratty, you wouldn't turn back! O dear, O dear!"

Recollection brought fresh waves of sorrow, and sobs again took full charge of him, preventing further speech.

The Rat stared straight in front of him, saying nothing, only patting Mole gently on the shoulder. After a time he muttered gloomily, "I see it all now! What a *pig* I have been! A pig – that's me! Just a pig – a plain pig!"

He waited till Mole's sobs became gradually less stormy and more rhythmical; he waited till at last sniffs were frequent and sobs only intermittent. Then he rose from his seat, and, remarking carelessly, "Well, now we'd really better be getting on, old chap!" set off up the road again, over the toilsome way they had come.

"Wherever are you (hic) going to (hic), Ratty?" cried the tearful Mole, looking up in alarm.

"We're going to find that home of yours, old fellow," replied the Rat pleasantly; "so you had better come along, for it will take some finding, and we shall want your nose."

"Oh, come back, Ratty, do!" cried the Mole, getting up and hurrying after him. "It's no good, I tell you! It's too late, and too dark, and the place is too far off, and the snow's coming! And – and I never meant to let you know I was feeling that way about it – it was all an accident and a mistake! And think of River Bank, and your supper!"

"Hang River Bank, and supper too!" said the Rat heartily. "I tell you, I'm going to find this place now, if I stay out all night. So cheer up, old chap, and take my arm, and we'll very soon be back there again."

Still snuffling, pleading, and reluctant, Mole suffered himself to be dragged back along the road by his imperious companion, who by a flow of cheerful talk and anecdote endeavoured to beguile his spirits back and make the weary way seem shorter. When at last it seemed to the Rat that they must be nearing that part of the road where the Mole had been "held up," he said, "Now, no more talking. Business! Use your nose, and give your mind to it."

They moved on in silence for some little way, when suddenly the Rat was conscious, through his arm that was linked in Mole's, of a faint sort of electric thrill that was passing down that animal's body. Instantly he disengaged himself, fell back a pace, and waited, all attention.

The signals were coming through!

Mole stood a moment rigid, while his uplifted nose, quivering slightly, felt the air.

Then a short, quick run forward – a fault – a check – a try back; and then a slow, steady, confident advance.

The Rat, much excited, kept close to his heels as the Mole, with something of the air of a sleep-walker, crossed a dry ditch, scrambled through a hedge, and nosed his way over a field open and trackless and bare in the faint starlight.

Suddenly, without giving warning, he dived; but the Rat was on the alert, and promptly followed him down the tunnel to which his unerring nose had faithfully led him.

It was close and airless, and the earthy smell was strong, and it seemed a long time to Rat ere the passage ended and he could stand erect and stretch and shake himself. The Mole struck a match, and by its light the Rat saw that they were standing in an open space, neatly swept and sanded underfoot, and directly facing them was Mole's little front door, with "Mole End" painted, in Gothic lettering, over the bell-pull at the side.

Mole reached down a lantern from a nail on the wail and lit it, and the Rat, looking round him, saw that they were in a sort of forecourt. A garden seat stood on one side of the door, and on the other a roller; for the Mole, who was a tidy animal when at home, could not stand having his ground kicked up by other animals into little runs that ended in earth-heaps. On the walls hung wire baskets with ferns in them, alternating with brackets carrying plaster statuary – Garibaldi, and the infant Samuel, and Queen Victoria, and other heroes of modern Italy. Down on one side of the forecourt ran a skittle-alley, with benches along it and little wooden tables marked with rings that hinted at beer-mugs. In the middle was a small round pond containing goldfish and surrounded by a cockle-shell border. Out of the centre of the pond rose a fanciful erection clothed in more cockle shells and topped by a large silvered glass ball that reflected everything all wrong and had a very pleasing effect.

Mole's face-beamed at the sight of all these objects so dear to him, and he hurried Rat through the door, lit a lamp in the hall, and took one glance round his old home. He saw the dust lying thick on everything, saw the cheerless, deserted look of the long-neglected house, and its narrow, meagre dimensions, its worn and shabby contents – and collapsed again on a hall-chair, his nose to his paws. "O Ratty!" he cried dismally, "why ever did I do it? Why did I bring you to this poor, cold little place, on a night like this, when you might have been at River Bank by this time, toasting your toes before a blazing fire, with all your own nice things about you!"

The Rat paid no heed to his doleful self-reproaches. He was running here and there, opening doors, inspecting rooms and cupboards, and lighting lamps and candles and sticking them, up everywhere. "What a capital little house this is!" he called out cheerily. "So compact! So well planned! Everything here and everything in its place! We'll make a jolly night of it. The first thing we want is a good fire; I'll see to that – I always know where to find things. So this is the parlour? Splendid! Your own idea, those little sleeping-bunks in the wall? Capital! Now, I'll fetch the wood and the coals, and you get a duster, Mole – you'll find one in the drawer of the kitchen table – and try and smarten things up a bit. Bustle about, old chap!"

Encouraged by his inspiriting companion, the Mole roused himself and dusted and polished with energy and heartiness, while the Rat, running to and fro with armfuls of fuel, soon had a cheerful blaze roaring up the chimney. He hailed the Mole to come and warm himself; but Mole promptly had another fit of the blues, dropping down on a couch in dark despair and burying his face in his duster. "Rat," he moaned, "how about your supper, you poor, cold, hungry, weary animal? I've nothing to give you – nothing – not a crumb!"

"What a fellow you are for giving in!" said the Rat reproachfully. "Why, only just now I saw a sardine-opener on the kitchen dresser, quite distinctly; and everybody knows that means there are sardines about somewhere in the neighbourhood. Rouse yourself! pull yourself together, and come with me and forage."

They went and foraged accordingly, hunting through every cupboard and turning out every drawer. The result was not so very depressing after all, though of course it might have been better; a tin of sardines – a box of captain's biscuits, nearly full – and a German sausage encased in silver paper.

"There's a banquet for you!" observed the Rat, as he arranged the table. "I know some animals who would give their ears to be sitting down to supper with us tonight!"

"No bread!" groaned the Mole dolorously; "no butter, no—"

"No *pâté de foie gras*, no champagne!" continued the Rat, grinning. "And that reminds me – what's that little door at the end of the passage? Your cellar, of course! Every luxury in this house! Just you wait a minute."

He made for the cellar door, and presently reappeared, somewhat dusty, with a bottle of beer in each paw and another under each arm, "Self-indulgent beggar you seem to be, Mole," he observed. "Deny yourself nothing. This is really the jolliest little place I ever was in. Now, wherever did you pick up those prints? Make the place look so home-like, they do. No wonder you're so fond of it, Mole. Tell us all about it, and how you came to make it what it is."

Then, while the Rat busied himself fetching plates, and knives and forks, and mustard which he mixed in an egg-cup, the Mole, his bosom still heaving with the stress of his recent emotion, related – somewhat shyly at first, but with more freedom as he warmed to his subject – how this was planned, and how that was thought out, and how this was got through a windfall from an aunt, and that was a wonderful find and a bargain, and this other thing was bought out of laborious savings and a certain amount of "going without." His spirits finally quite restored, he must needs go and caress his possessions, and take a lamp and show off their points to his visitor and expatiate on them, quite forgetful of the supper they both so much needed; Rat, who was desperately hungry but strove to conceal it, nodding seriously, examining with a puckered brow, and saying, "wonderful," and "most remarkable," at intervals, when the chance for an observation was given him.

At last the Rat succeeded in decoying him to the table, and had just got seriously to work with the sardine-opener when sounds were heard from the fore-court without – sounds like the scuffling of small feet in the gravel and a confused murmur of tiny voices, while broken sentences reached them – "Now, all in a line – hold the lantern up a bit, Tommy – clear your throats first – no coughing after I say one, two, three. – Where's young Bill? – Here, come on, do, we're all a-waiting—"

"What's up?" inquired the Rat, pausing in his labours.

"I think it must be the field mice," replied the Mole, with a touch of pride in his manner. "They go round carol singing regularly at this time of the year. They're quite an institution in these parts. And they never pass me over – they come to Mole End last of all; and I used to give them hot drinks, and supper too sometimes, when I could afford it. It will be like old times to hear them again."

"Let's have a look at them!" cried the Rat, jumping up and running to the door.

It was a pretty sight, and a seasonable one, that met their eyes when they flung the door open. In the forecourt, lit by the dim rays of a horn lantern, some eight or ten little field mice stood in a semicircle, red worsted comforters round their throats, their forepaws thrust deep into their pockets, their feet jigging for warmth. With bright beady eyes they glanced shyly at each other, sniggering a little, sniffing and applying coat-sleeves a good deal. As the door opened, one of the elder ones that carried the lantern was just saying, "Now then, one, two, three!" and forthwith their shrill little voices uprose on the air, singing one of the old-time carols that their forefathers composed in fields that were fallow and held by frost, or when snowbound in chimney corners, and handed down to be sung in the miry street to lamplit windows at Yule-time.

CAROL

Villagers all, this frosty tide,
Let your doors swing open wide,
Though wind may follow, and snow beside,
Yet draw us in by your fire to bide;
    Joy shall be yours in the morning!

Here we stand in the cold and the sleet,
Blowing fingers and stamping feet,
Come from far away you to greet—
You by the fire and we in the street—
    Bidding you joy in the morning!

For ere one half of the night was gone,
Sudden a star has led us on,
Raining bliss and benison—
Bliss tomorrow and more anon,
    Joy for every morning!

Goodman Joseph toiled through the snow—
Saw the star o'er a stable low;
Mary she might not further go—
Welcome thatch, and litter below!
    Joy was hers in the morning!

And then they heard the angels tell
Who were the first to cry Nowell?
Animals all, as it befell,
In the stable where they did dwell!
    Joy shall be theirs in the morning!

The voices ceased, the singers, bashful but smiling, exchanged sidelong glances, and silence succeeded – but for a moment only. Then, from up above and far away, down the tunnel they had so lately travelled was borne to their ears in a faint musical hum the sound of distant bells ringing a joyful and clangorous peal.

"Very well sung, boys!" cried the Rat heartily. "And now come along in, all of you, and warm yourselves by the fire, and have something hot!"

"Yes, come along, field mice," cried the Mole eagerly. "This is quite like old times! Shut the door after you. Pull up that settle to the fire. Now, you just wait a minute, while we – O, Ratty!" he cried in despair, plumping down on a seat, with tears impending. "Whatever are we doing? We've nothing to give them!"

"You leave all that to me," said the masterful Rat. "Here, you with the lantern! Come over this way. I want to talk to you. Now, tell me, are there any shops open at this hour of the night?"

"Why, certainly, sir," replied the field mouse respectfully. "At this time of the year our shops keep open to all sorts of hours."

"Then look here!" said the Rat. "You go off at once, you and your lantern, and you get me—"

existence. He did not at all want to abandon the new life and its splendid spaces, to turn his back on sun and air and all they offered him and creep home and stay there; the upper world was all too strong, it called to him still, even down there, and he knew he must return to the larger stage. But it was good to think he had this to come back to; this place which was all his own, these things which were so glad to see him again and could always be counted upon for the same simple welcome.

"Doing Good"

from *The Phoenix and the Carpet* by E Nesbit

The Phoenix and the Carpet is the second in a trilogy of novels by E Nesbit, which started with the classic book Five Children and It. In this story, the five children – Cyril, Anthea, Robert, Jane and the Lamb – discover a talking phoenix who grants them three wishes a day through the use of a magic carpet, and they embark on a series of adventures together.

Early on in the book, the children travel to the coast of France, where the carpet takes them to a mysterious tower. Beneath the tower they discover a hidden underground passage that leads them to a room full of sacks of golden coins! But in their rush to escape, they accidentally leave the treasure behind.

As the following chapter begins, the children are facing the prospect of being separated from the Phoenix while they spend the festive period with their aunt. They decide that there is time for one last adventure before they go, but like the March sisters in *Little Women*, they also agree that "there's something about Christmas that makes you want to do good", and so they propose to find a place where they can do something nice for somebody else. . .

"We shan't be able to go anywhere on the carpet for a whole week, though," said Robert.

"And I'm glad of it," said Jane, unexpectedly.

"Glad?" said Cyril; "*Glad?*"

It was breakfast-time, and mother's letter, telling them how they were all going for Christmas to their aunt's at Lyndhurst, and how father and mother would meet them there, having been read by everyone, lay on the table, drinking hot bacon-fat with one corner and eating marmalade with the other.

"Yes, glad," said Jane. "I don't want any more things to happen just now. I feel like you do when you've been to three parties in a week – like we did at granny's once – and extras in between, toys and chocs and things like that. I want everything to be just real, and no fancy things happening at all."

"I don't like being obliged to keep things from mother," said Anthea. "I don't know why, but it makes me feel selfish and mean."

"If we could only get the mater to believe it, we might take her to the jolliest places," said Cyril, thoughtfully. "As it is, we've just got to be selfish and mean – if it is that – but I don't feel it is."

"I *know* it isn't, but I *feel* it is," said Anthea, "and that's just as bad."

"It's worse," said Robert; "if you knew it and didn't feel it, it wouldn't matter so much."

"That's being a hardened criminal, father says," put in Cyril, and he picked up mother's letter and wiped its corners with his handkerchief, to whose colour a trifle of bacon-fat and marmalade made but little difference.

"We're going tomorrow, anyhow," said Robert. "don't," he added, with a good-boy expression on his face – "don't let's be ungrateful for our blessings; don't let's waste the day in saying how horrid it is to keep secrets from mother, when we all know Anthea tried all she knew to give her the secret, and she wouldn't take it. Let's get on the carpet and have a jolly good wish. You'll have time enough to repent of things all next week."

"Yes," said Cyril, "let's. It's not really wrong."

"Well, look here," said Anthea. "You know there's something about Christmas that makes you want to be good – however little you wish it at other times. Couldn't we wish the carpet to take us somewhere where we should have the chance to do some good and kind action? It would be an adventure just the same," she pleaded.

"I don't mind," said Cyril. "We shan't know where we're going, and that'll be exciting. No one knows what'll happen. We'd best put on our outers in case—"

"We might rescue a traveller buried in the snow, like St Bernard dogs, with barrels round our necks," said Jane, beginning to be interested.

"Or we might arrive just in time to witness a will being signed – more tea, please," said Robert, "and we should see the old man hide it away in the secret cupboard; and then, after long years, when the rightful heir was in despair, we should lead him to the hidden panel and—"

"Yes," interrupted Anthea; "or we might be taken to some freezing garret in a German town, where a poor little pale, sick child—"

"We haven't any German money," interrupted Cyril, "so *that's* no go. What I should like would be getting into the middle of a war and getting hold of secret intelligence and taking it to the general, and he would make me a lieutenant or a scout, or a hussar."

When breakfast was cleared away, Anthea swept the carpet, and the children sat down on it, together with the Phoenix, who had been especially invited, as a Christmas treat, to come with them and witness the good and kind action they were about to do.

Four children and one bird were ready, and the wish was wished.

Everyone closed its eyes, so as to feel the topsy-turvy swirl of the carpet's movement as little as possible.

When the eyes were opened again the children found themselves on the carpet, and the carpet was in its proper place on the floor of their own nursery at Camden Town.

"I say," said Cyril, "here's a go!"

"Do you think it's worn out? The wishing part of it, I mean?" Robert anxiously asked the Phoenix.

"It's not that," said the Phoenix; "but – well – what did you wish—?"

"Oh! I see what it means," said Robert, with deep disgust; "it's like the end of a fairy story in a Sunday magazine. How perfectly beastly!"

"You mean it means we can do kind and good actions where we are? I see. I suppose it wants us to carry coals for the cook or make clothes for the bare heathens. Well, I simply won't. And the last day and everything. Look here!" Cyril spoke loudly and firmly. "We want to go somewhere really interesting, where we have a chance of doing something good and kind; we don't want to do it here, but somewhere else. See? Now, then."

The obedient carpet started instantly, and the four children and one bird fell in a heap together, and as they fell were plunged in perfect darkness.

"Are you all there?" said Anthea, breathlessly, through the black dark. Everyone owned that it was there.

"Where are we? Oh! how shivery and wet it is! Ugh! – oh! – I've put my hand in a puddle!"

"Has anyone got any matches?" said Anthea, hopelessly. She felt sure that no one would have any.

It was then that Robert, with a radiant smile of triumph that was quite wasted in the darkness, where, of course, no one could see anything, drew out of his pocket a box of matches, struck a match and lighted a candle – two candles. And everyone, with its mouth open, blinked at the sudden light.

"Well done, Bobs," said his sisters, and even Cyril's

natural brotherly feelings could not check his admiration of Robert's foresight.

"I've always carried them about ever since the lone tower day," said Robert, with modest pride. "I knew we should want them some day. I kept the secret well, didn't I?"

"Oh, yes," said Cyril, with fine scorn. "I found them the Sunday after, when I was feeling in your Norfolks for the knife you borrowed off me. But I thought you'd only sneaked them for Chinese lanterns, or reading in bed by."

"Bobs," said Anthea, suddenly, "do you know where we are? This is the underground passage, and look there – there's the money and the money-bags, and everything."

By this time the ten eyes had got used to the light of the candles, and no one could help seeing that Anthea spoke the truth.

"It seems an odd place to do good and kind acts in, though," said Jane. "There's no one to do them to."

"Don't you be too sure," said Cyril; "just round the next turning we might find a prisoner who has languished here for years and years, and we could take him out on our carpet and restore him to his sorrowing friends."

"Of course we could," said Robert, standing up and holding the candle above his head to see further off; "or we might find the bones of a poor prisoner and take them to his friends to be buried properly – that's always a kind action in books, though I never could see what bones matter."

"I wish you wouldn't," said Jane.

"I know exactly where we shall find the bones, too," Robert went on. "You see that dark arch just along the passage? Well, just inside there—"

"If you don't stop going on like that," said Jane, firmly, "I shall scream, and then I'll faint – so now then!"

"And I will, too," said Anthea.

Robert was not pleased at being checked in his flight of fancy.

"You girls will never be great writers," he said bitterly. "They just love to think of things in dungeons, and chains, and knobbly bare human bones, and—"

Jane had opened her mouth to scream, but before she could decide how you began when you wanted to faint, the golden voice of the Phoenix spoke through the gloom.

"Peace!" it said; "there are no bones here except the small but useful sets that you have inside you. And you did not invite me to come out with you to hear you talk about bones, but to see you do some good and kind action."

"We can't do it here," said Robert, sulkily.

"No," rejoined the bird. "The only thing we can do here, it seems, is to try to frighten our little sisters."

"He didn't, really, and I'm not so *very* little," said Jane, rather ungratefully.

Robert was silent. It was Cyril who suggested that perhaps they had better take the money and go.

"That wouldn't be a kind act, except to ourselves; and it wouldn't be good, whatever way you look at it," said Anthea, "to take money that's not ours."

"We might take it and spend it all on benefits to the poor and aged," said Cyril.

"That wouldn't make it right to steal," said Anthea, stoutly.

"I don't know," said Cyril. They were all standing up now. "Stealing is taking things that belong to someone else, and there's no one else."

"It can't be stealing if—"

"That's right," said Robert, with ironical approval; "stand here all day arguing while the candles burn out. You'll like it awfully when it's all dark again – and bony."

"Let's get out, then," said Anthea. "We can argue as we go." So they rolled up the carpet and went. But when they had crept along to the place where the passage led into the topless tower they found the way blocked by a great stone, which they could not move.

"There!" said Robert. "I hope you're satisfied!"

"Everything has two ends," said the Phoenix, softly; "even a quarrel or a secret passage."

So they turned round and went back, and Robert was made to go first with one of the candles, because he was the one who had begun to talk about bones. And Cyril carried the carpet.

"I wish you hadn't put bones into our heads," said Jane, as they went along.

"I didn't; you always had them. More bones than brains," said Robert.

The passage was long, and there were arches and steps and turnings and dark alcoves that the girls did not much like passing. The passage ended in a flight of steps. Robert went up them.

Suddenly he staggered heavily back on to the following feet of Jane, and everybody screamed, "Oh! what is it?"

"I've only bashed my head in," said Robert, when he

had groaned for some time; "that's all. Don't mention it; I like it. The stairs just go right slap into the ceiling, and it's a stone ceiling. You can't do good and kind actions underneath a paving-stone."

"Stairs aren't made to lead just to paving-stones as a general rule," said the Phoenix. "Put your shoulder to the wheel."

"There isn't any wheel," said the injured Robert, still rubbing his head.

But Cyril had pushed past him to the top stair, and was already shoving his hardest against the stone above. Of course, it did not give in the least.

"If it's a trap-door—" said Cyril. And he stopped shoving and began to feel about with his hands.

"Yes, there is a bolt. I can't move it."

By a happy chance Cyril had in his pocket the oil-can of his father's bicycle; he put the carpet down at the foot of the stairs, and he lay on his back, with his head on the top step and his feet straggling down among his young relations, and he oiled the bolt till the drops of rust and oil fell down on his face. One even went into his mouth – open, as he panted with the exertion of keeping up this unnatural position. Then he tried again, but still the bolt would not move. So now he tied his handkerchief –

the one with the bacon-fat and marmalade on it – to the bolt, and Robert's handkerchief to that, in a reef knot, which cannot come undone however much you pull, and, indeed, gets tighter and tighter the more you pull it. This must not be confused with a granny knot, which comes undone if you look at it. And then he and Robert pulled, and the girls put their arms round their brothers and pulled too, and suddenly the bolt gave way with a rusty scrunch, and they all rolled together to the bottom of the stairs – all but the Phoenix, which had taken to its wings when the pulling began.

Nobody was hurt much, because the rolled-up carpet broke their fall; and now, indeed, the shoulders of the boys were used to some purpose, for the stone allowed them to heave it up. They felt it give; dust fell freely on them.

"Now, then," cried Robert, forgetting his head and his temper, "push all together. One, two, three!"

The stone was heaved up. It swung up on a creaking, unwilling hinge, and showed a growing oblong of dazzling daylight; and it fell back with a bang against something that kept it upright. Everyone climbed out, but there was not room for everyone to stand comfortably in the little paved house where they found themselves, so when the Phoenix had fluttered up from the darkness they let the stone down, and it closed like a trap-door, as indeed it was.

You can have no idea how dusty and dirty the children were. Fortunately there was no one to see them but each other. The place they were in was a little shrine, built on the side of a road that went winding up through yellow-green fields to the topless tower. Below them were fields and orchards, all bare boughs and brown furrows, and little houses and gardens. The shrine was a kind of tiny chapel with no front wall – just a place for people to stop and rest in and wish to be good. So the Phoenix told them. There was an image that had once been brightly coloured, but the rain and snow had beaten in through the open front of the shrine, and the poor image was dull and weather-stained. Under it was written: "*St Jean de Luz. Priez pour nous.*" It was a sad little place, very neglected and lonely, and yet it was nice, Anthea thought, that poor travellers should come to this little rest-house in the hurry and worry of their journeyings and be quiet for a few minutes, and think about being good. The thought of St Jean de Luz – who had, no doubt, in his time, been very good and kind – made Anthea want more than ever to do something kind and good.

"Tell us," she said to the Phoenix, "what is the good and kind action the carpet brought us here to do?"

"I think it would be kind to find the owners of the treasure and tell them about it," said Cyril.

"And give it them *all*?" said Jane.

"Yes. But whose is it?"

"I should go to the first house and ask the name of the owner of the castle," said the golden bird, and really the idea seemed a good one.

They dusted each other as well as they could and went down the road. A little way on they found a tiny spring, bubbling out of the hillside and falling into a rough stone basin surrounded by draggled hart's-tongue ferns, now hardly green at all. Here the children washed their hands and faces and dried them on their pocket-handkerchiefs, which always, on these occasions, seem unnaturally small. Cyril's and Robert's handkerchiefs, indeed, rather undid the effects of the wash. But in spite of this the party certainly looked cleaner than before.

The first house they came to was a little white house with green shutters and a slate roof. It stood in a prim little garden, and down each side of the neat path were large stone vases for flowers to grow in; but all the flowers were dead now.

Along one side of the house was a sort of wide veranda, built of poles and trellis-work, and a vine crawled all over it. It was wider than our English verandas, and Anthea thought it must look lovely when the green leaves and the grapes were there; but now there were only dry, reddish-brown stalks and stems, with a few withered leaves caught in them.

The children walked up to the front door. It was green and narrow. A chain with a handle hung beside it, and joined itself quite openly to a rusty bell that hung under the porch. Cyril had pulled the bell and its noisy clang was dying away before the terrible thought came to all. Cyril spoke it.

"My hat!" he breathed. "We don't know any French!"

At this moment the door opened. A very tall, lean lady, with pale ringlets like whitey-brown paper or oak shavings, stood before them. She had an ugly grey dress and a black silk apron. Her eyes were small and grey and not pretty, and the rims were red, as though she had been crying.

She addressed the party in something that sounded like a foreign language, and ended with something which they were sure was a question. Of course, no one could answer it.

"What does she say?" Robert asked, looking down into the hollow of his jacket, where the Phoenix was nestling. But before the Phoenix could answer, the whitey-brown lady's face was lighted up by a most charming smile.

"You – you ar-r-re fr-r-rom the England!" she cried. "I love so much the England. *Mais entrez – entrez donc tous!* Enter, then – enter all. One *essuyes* his feet on the carpet." She pointed to the mat.

"We only wanted to ask—"

"I shall say you all that what you wish," said the lady. "Enter only!"

So they all went in, wiping their feet on a very clean mat, and putting the carpet in a safe corner of the veranda.

"The most beautiful days of my life," said the lady, as she shut the door, 'did pass themselves in England. And since long time I have not heard an English voice to repeal me the past."

This warm welcome embarrassed every one, but most the boys, for the floor of the hall was of such very clean red and white tiles, and the floor of the sitting-room so very shiny – like a black looking-glass – that each felt as though he had on far more boots than usual, and far noisier.

There was a wood fire, very small and very bright, on the hearth – neat little logs laid on brass fire-dogs. Some portraits of powdered ladies and gentlemen hung in oval frames on the pale walls. There were silver candlesticks on the mantelpiece, and there were chairs and a table, very slim and polite, with slender legs. The room was extremely bare, but with a bright foreign bareness that was very cheerful, in an odd way of its own. At the end of the polished table a very un-English little boy sat on a footstool in a high-backed, uncomfortable-looking chair. He wore black velvet, and the kind of collar – all frills and lacey – that Robert would rather have died than wear; but then the little French boy was much younger than Robert.

"Oh, how pretty!" said everyone. But no one meant the little French boy, with the velvety short knickerbockers and the velvety short hair.

What everyone admired was a little, little Christmas tree, very green, and standing in a very red little flowerpot, and hung round with very bright little things made of tinsel and coloured paper. There were tiny candles on the tree, but they were not lighted yet.

"But yes – is it not that it is genteel?" said the lady. "Sit down you then, and let us see."

The children sat down in a row on the stiff chairs against the wall, and the lady lighted a long, slim red taper at the wood flame, and then she drew the curtains and lit the little candles, and when they were all lighted the little French boy suddenly shouted, *"Bravo, ma tante! Oh, que c'est gentil,"* and the English children shouted "Hooray!"

Then there was a struggle in the breast of Robert, and out fluttered the Phoenix – spread his gold wings, flew to the top of the Christmas tree, and perched there.

"Ah! catch it, then," cried the lady; "it will itself burn – your genteel parrakeet!"

"It won't," said Robert, "thank you."

And the little French boy clapped his clean and tidy hands; but the lady was so anxious that the Phoenix fluttered down and walked up and down on the shiny walnut-wood table.

"Is it that it talks?" asked the lady.

And the Phoenix replied in excellent French. It said, *"Parfaitement, madame!"*

"Oh, the pretty parrakeet," said the lady. "Can it say still of other things?"

And the Phoenix replied, this time in English, "Why are you sad so near Christmastime?"

The children looked at it with one gasp of horror and surprise, for the youngest of them knew that it is far from manners to notice that strangers have been crying, and much worse to ask them the reason of their tears. And, of course, the lady began to cry again, very much indeed, after calling the Phoenix a bird without a heart; and she could not find her handkerchief, so Anthea offered hers, which was still very damp and no use at all. She also hugged the lady, and this seemed to be of more use than the handkerchief, so that presently the lady stopped crying, and found her own handkerchief and dried her eyes, and called Anthea a cherished angel.

"I am sorry we came just when you were so sad," said Anthea, "but we really only wanted to ask you whose that castle is on the hill."

"Oh, my little angel," said the poor lady, sniffing, "today and for hundreds of years the castle is to us, to our family. Tomorrow it must that I sell it to some strangers – and my little Henri, who ignores all, he will not have never the lands paternal. But what will you? His father, my brother – Mr the Marquis – has spent much of money, and it the must, despite the sentiments of familial respect, that I admit that my sainted father he also—"

"How would you feel if you found a lot of money – hundreds and thousands of gold pieces?" asked Cyril.

The lady smiled sadly.

"Ah! one has already recounted to you the legend?" she said. "It is true that one says that it is long time; oh! but long time, one of our ancestors has hid a treasure – of gold, and of gold, and of gold – enough to enrich my little Henri for the life. But all that, my children, it is but the accounts of fays—"

"She means fairy stories," whispered the Phoenix to Robert. "Tell her what you have found."

So Robert told, while Anthea and Jane hugged the lady for fear she should faint for joy, like people in books, and they hugged her with the earnest, joyous hugs of unselfish delight.

"It's no use explaining how we got in," said Robert, when he had told of the finding of the treasure, "because you would find it a little difficult to understand, and much more difficult to believe. But we can show you where the gold is and help you to fetch it away."

The lady looked doubtfully at Robert as she absently returned the hugs of the girls.

"No, he's not making it up," said Anthea; "it's true, TRUE, TRUE! – and we are so glad."

"You would not be capable to torment an old woman?" she said; "and it is not possible that it be a dream."

"It really IS true," said Cyril; "and I congratulate you very much."

His tone of studied politeness seemed to convince more than the raptures of the others.

"If I do not dream," she said, "Henri come to Manon – and you – you shall come all with me to Mr the Curate. Is it not?"

Manon was a wrinkled old woman with a red and yellow handkerchief twisted round her head. She took Henri, who was already sleepy with the excitement of his Christmas tree and his visitors, and when the lady had put on a stiff black cape and a wonderful black silk bonnet and a pair of black wooden clogs over her black cashmere house-boots, the whole party went down the road to a little white house – very like the one they had left – where an old priest, with a good face, welcomed them with a politeness so great that it hid his astonishment.

The lady, with her French waving hands and her shrugging French shoulders and her trembling French speech, told the story. And now the priest, who knew no English, shrugged *his* shoulders and waved *his* hands and spoke also in French.

"He thinks," whispered the Phoenix, "that her troubles have turned her brain. What a pity you know no French!"

"I do know a lot of French," whispered Robert, indignantly; "but it's all about the pencil of the gardener's son and the penknife of the baker's niece – nothing that anyone ever wants to say."

"If *I* speak," the bird whispered, "he'll think HE's mad, too."

"Tell me what to say."

"Say 'C'est vrai, monsieur. Venez donc voir,'" said the Phoenix; and then Robert earned the undying respect of everybody by suddenly saying, very loudly and distinctly—

"Say vray, mossoo; venny dong vwaw."

The priest was disappointed when he found that Robert's French began and ended with these useful words; but, at any rate, he saw that if the lady was mad she was not the only one, and he put on a big beavery hat, and got a candle and matches and a spade, and they all went up the hill to the wayside shrine of St John of Luz.

"Now," said Robert, "I will go first and show you where it is."

So they prised the stone up with a corner of the spade, and Robert did go first, and they all followed and found the golden treasure exactly as they had left it. And everyone was flushed with the joy of performing such a wonderfully kind action.

Then the lady and the priest clasped hands and wept for joy, as French people do, and knelt down and touched the money, and talked very fast and both together, and the lady embraced all the children three times each, and called them "little garden angels," and then she and the priest shook each other by both hands again, and talked, and talked, and talked, faster and more Frenchy than you would have believed possible. And the children were struck dumb with joy and pleasure.

"Get away NOW," said the Phoenix softly, breaking in on the radiant dream.

So the children crept away, and out through the little shrine, and the lady and the priest were so tearfully, talkatively happy that they never noticed that the guardian angels had gone.

The "garden angels" ran down the hill to the lady's little house, where they had left the carpet on the veranda, and they spread it out and said "Home," and no one saw them disappear, except little Henri, who had flattened his nose into a white button against the window-glass, and when he tried to tell his aunt she thought he had been dreaming. So that was all right. "It is much the best thing we've done," said Anthea, when they talked it over at tea-time. "In the future we'll only do kind actions with the carpet."

"Ahem!" said the Phoenix.

"I beg your pardon?" said Anthea.

"Oh, nothing," said the bird. "I was only thinking!"

"Matthew Insists on Puffed Sleeves"
from *Anne of Green Gables* by L M Montgomery

Sometimes at Christmas we go to extraordinary lengths to make the people we care about us happy, as this chapter from L. M. Montgomery's *Anne of Green Gables* shows.

As the book begins, Matthew and Marilla Cuthbert have decided to adopt an orphan boy to help them out on Green Gables – their farm in Nova Scotia, Canada. However, due to a mix-up, the orphanage sends along a girl called Anne instead. Although they initially consider sending her back, they soon come to care deeply for Anne – so much so that, come Christmastime, Matthew is determined that she should have a nice dress, in spite of the fact that he knows nothing about women's clothing at all.

Matthew was having a bad ten minutes of it. He had come into the kitchen, in the twilight of a cold, grey December evening, and had sat down in the wood-box corner to take off his heavy boots, unconscious of the fact that Anne and a bevy of her schoolmates were having a practice of "The Fairy Queen" in the sitting room. Presently they came trooping through the hall and out into the kitchen, laughing and chattering gaily. They did not see Matthew, who shrank bashfully back into the shadows beyond the wood-box with a boot in one hand and a bootjack in the other, and he watched them shyly for the aforesaid ten minutes as they put on caps and jackets and talked about the dialogue and the concert. Anne stood among them, bright eyed and animated as they; but Matthew suddenly became conscious that there was something about her different from her mates. And what worried Matthew was that the difference impressed him as being something that should not exist. Anne had a brighter face, and bigger, starrier eyes, and more delicate features than the other; even shy, unobservant Matthew had learned to take note of these things; but the difference that disturbed him did not consist in any of these respects. Then in what did it consist?

Matthew was haunted by this question long after the girls had gone, arm in arm, down the long, hard-frozen lane and Anne had betaken herself to her books. He could not refer it to Marilla, who, he felt, would be quite sure to sniff scornfully and remark that the only difference she saw between Anne and the other girls was that they sometimes kept their tongues quiet while Anne never did. This, Matthew felt, would be no great help.

He had recourse to his pipe that evening to help him study it out, much to Marilla's disgust. After two hours of smoking and hard reflection Matthew arrived at a solution of his problem. Anne was not dressed like the other girls!

The more Matthew thought about the matter the more he was convinced that Anne never had been dressed like the other girls – never since she had come to Green Gables. Marilla kept her clothed in plain, dark dresses, all made after the same unvarying pattern. If Matthew knew there was such a thing as fashion in dress it was as much as he did; but he was quite sure that Anne's sleeves did not look at all like the sleeves the other girls wore. He recalled the cluster of little girls he had seen around her that evening – all gay in waists of red and blue and pink and white – and he wondered why Marilla always kept her so plainly and soberly gowned.

Of course, it must be all right. Marilla knew best and Marilla was bringing her up. Probably some wise, inscrutable motive was to be served thereby. But surely it would do no harm to let the child have one pretty dress – something like Diana Barry always wore. Matthew decided that he would give her one; that surely could not be objected to as an unwarranted putting in of his oar. Christmas was only a fortnight off. A nice new dress would be the very thing for a present. Matthew, with a sigh of satisfaction, put away his pipe and went to bed, while Marilla opened all the doors and aired the house.

The very next evening Matthew betook himself to

Carmody to buy the dress, determined to get the worst over and have done with it. It would be, he felt assured, no trifling ordeal. There were some things Matthew could buy and prove himself no mean bargainer; but he knew he would be at the mercy of shopkeepers when it came to buying a girl's dress.

After much cogitation Matthew resolved to go to Samuel Lawson's store instead of William Blair's. To be sure, the Cuthberts always had gone to William Blair's; it was almost as much a matter of conscience with them as to attend the Presbyterian church and vote Conservative. But William Blair's two daughters frequently waited on customers there and Matthew held them in absolute dread. He could contrive to deal with them when he knew exactly what he wanted and could point it out; but in such a matter as this, requiring explanation and consultation, Matthew felt that he must be sure of a man behind the counter. So he would go to Lawson's, where Samuel or his son would wait on him.

Alas! Matthew did not know that Samuel, in the recent expansion of his business, had set up a lady clerk also; she was a niece of his wife's and a very dashing young person indeed, with a huge, drooping pompadour, big, rolling brown eyes, and a most extensive and bewildering smile. She was dressed with exceeding smartness and wore several bangle bracelets that glittered and rattled and tinkled with every movement of her hands. Matthew was covered with confusion at finding her there at all; and those bangles completely wrecked his wits at one fell swoop.

"What can I do for you this evening, Mr Cuthbert?" Miss Lucilla Harris inquired, briskly and ingratiatingly, tapping the counter with both hands.

"Have you any – any – any – well now, say any garden rakes?" stammered Matthew.

Miss Harris looked somewhat surprised, as well she might, to hear a man inquiring for garden rakes in the middle of December.

"I believe we have one or two left over," she said, "but they're upstairs in the lumber room. I'll go and see." During her absence Matthew collected his scattered senses for another effort.

When Miss Harris returned with the rake and cheerfully inquired: "Anything else tonight, Mr Cuthbert?" Matthew took his courage in both hands and replied: "Well now, since you suggest it, I might as well – take – that is – look at – buy some – some hayseed."

Miss Harris had heard Matthew Cuthbert called odd. She now concluded that he was entirely crazy.

"We only keep hayseed in the spring," she explained loftily. "We've none on hand just now."

"Oh, certainly – certainly – just as you say," stammered unhappy Matthew, seizing the rake and making for the door. At the threshold he recollected that he had not paid for it and he turned miserably back. While Miss Harris was counting out his change he rallied his powers for a final desperate attempt.

"Well now – if it isn't too much trouble – I might as well – that is – I'd like to look at – at – some sugar."

"White or brown?" queried Miss Harris patiently.

"Oh – well now – brown," said Matthew feebly.

"There's a barrel of it over there," said Miss Harris, shaking her bangles at it. "It's the only kind we have."

"I'll – I'll take twenty pounds of it," said Matthew, with beads of perspiration standing on his forehead.

Matthew had driven halfway home before he was his own man again. It had been a gruesome experience, but it served him right, he thought, for committing the heresy of going to a strange store. When he reached home he hid the rake in the tool house, but the sugar he carried in to Marilla.

"Brown sugar!" exclaimed Marilla. "Whatever possessed you to get so much? You know I never use it except for the hired man's porridge or black fruit cake. Jerry's gone and I've made my cake long ago. It's not good sugar, either – it's coarse and dark – William Blair doesn't usually keep sugar like that."

"I – I thought it might come in handy sometime," said Matthew, making good his escape.

When Matthew came to think the matter over he decided that a woman was required to cope with the situation. Marilla was out of the question. Matthew felt sure she would throw cold water on his project at once. Remained only Mrs Lynde; for of no other woman in Avonlea would Matthew have dared to ask advice. To Mrs Lynde he went accordingly, and that good lady promptly took the matter out of the harassed man's hands.

"Pick out a dress for you to give Anne? To be sure I will. I'm going to Carmody tomorrow and I'll attend to it. Have you something particular in mind? No? Well, I'll just go by my own judgement then. I believe a nice rich brown would just suit Anne, and William Blair has some new gloria in that's real pretty. Perhaps you'd like me to make it up for her, too, seeing that if Marilla was to make it Anne would probably get wind of it before the time and spoil the surprise? Well, I'll do it. No, it isn't a mite of trouble. I like sewing. I'll make it to fit my niece, Jenny Gillis, for she and Anne are as like as two peas as far as figure goes."

"Well now, I'm much obliged," said Matthew, "and – and – I dunno – but I'd like – I think they make the sleeves different nowadays to what they used to be. If it wouldn't be asking too much I – I'd like them made in the new way."

"Puffs? Of course. You needn't worry a speck more about it, Matthew. I'll make it up in the very latest fashion," said Mrs Lynde. To herself she added when Matthew had gone:

"It'll be a real satisfaction to see that poor child wearing something decent for once. The way Marilla dresses her is positively ridiculous, that's what, and I've ached to tell her so plainly a dozen times. I've held my tongue though, for I can see Marilla doesn't want advice and she thinks she knows more about bringing children up than I do for all she's an old maid. But that's always the way. Folks that has brought up children know that there's no hard and fast method in the world that'll suit every child. But them as never have think it's all as plain and easy as Rule of Three – just set your three terms down so fashion, and the sum'll work out correct. But flesh and blood don't come under the head of arithmetic and that's where Marilla Cuthbert makes her mistake. I suppose she's trying to cultivate a spirit of humility in Anne by dressing her as she does; but it's more likely to cultivate envy and discontent. I'm sure the child must feel the difference between her clothes and the other girls'. But to think of Matthew taking notice of it! That man is waking up after being asleep for over sixty years."

Marilla knew all the following fortnight that Matthew had something on his mind, but what it was she could not guess, until Christmas Eve, when Mrs Lynde brought up the new dress. Marilla behaved pretty well on the whole, although it is very likely she distrusted Mrs Lynde's diplomatic explanation that she had made the dress because Matthew was afraid Anne would find out about it too soon if Marilla made it.

"So this is what Matthew has been looking so mysterious over and grinning about to himself for two weeks, is it?" she said a little stiffly but tolerantly. "I knew he was up to some foolishness. Well, I must say I don't think Anne needed any more dresses. I made her three good, warm, serviceable ones this fall, and anything more is sheer extravagance. There's enough material in those sleeves alone to make a waist, I declare there is. You'll just pamper Anne's vanity, Matthew, and she's as vain as a peacock now. Well, I hope she'll be satisfied at last, for I know she's been hankering after those silly sleeves ever since they came in, although she never said a word after the first. The puffs have been getting bigger and more ridiculous right along; they're as big as balloons now. Next year anybody who wears them will have to go through a door sideways."

Christmas morning broke on a beautiful white world. It had been a very mild December and people had looked forward to a green Christmas; but just enough snow fell softly in the night to transfigure Avonlea. Anne peeped out from her frosted gable window with delighted eyes. The firs in the Haunted Wood were all feathery and wonderful; the birches and wild cherry trees were outlined in pearl; the ploughed fields were stretches of snowy dimples; and there was a crisp tang in the air that was glorious. Anne ran downstairs singing until her voice re-echoed through Green Gables.

"Merry Christmas, Marilla! Merry Christmas,

Matthew! Isn't it a lovely Christmas? I'm so glad it's white. Any other kind of Christmas doesn't seem real, does it? I don't like green Christmases. They're not green – they're just nasty faded browns and greys. What makes people call them green? Why – why – Matthew, is that for me? Oh, Matthew!"

Matthew had sheepishly unfolded the dress from its paper swathings and held it out with a deprecatory glance at Marilla, who feigned to be contemptuously filling the teapot, but nevertheless watched the scene out of the corner of her eye with a rather interested air.

Anne took the dress and looked at it in reverent silence. Oh, how pretty it was – a lovely soft brown gloria with all the gloss of silk; a skirt with dainty frills and shirrings; a waist elaborately pintucked in the most fashionable way, with a little ruffle of filmy lace at the neck. But the sleeves – they were the crowning glory! Long elbow cuffs, and above them two beautiful puffs divided by rows of shirring and bows of brown-silk ribbon.

"That's a Christmas present for you, Anne," said Matthew shyly. "Why – why – Anne, don't you like it? Well now – well now."

For Anne's eyes had suddenly filled with tears.

"*Like* it! Oh, Matthew!" Anne laid the dress over a chair and clasped her hands. "Matthew, it's perfectly exquisite. Oh, I can never thank you enough. Look at those sleeves! Oh, it seems to me this must be a happy dream."

"Well, well, let us have breakfast," interrupted Marilla. "I must say, Anne, I don't think you needed the dress; but since Matthew has got it for you, see that you take good care of it. There's a hair ribbon Mrs Lynde left for you. It's brown, to match the dress. Come now, sit in."

"I don't see how I'm going to eat breakfast," said Anne rapturously. "Breakfast seems so commonplace at such an exciting moment. I'd rather feast my eyes on that dress. I'm so glad that puffed sleeves are still fashionable. It did seem to me that I'd never get over it if they went out before I had a dress with them. I'd never have felt quite satisfied, you see. It was lovely of Mrs Lynde to give me the ribbon too. I feel that I ought to be a very good girl indeed. It's at times like this I'm sorry I'm not a model little girl; and I always resolve that I will be in future. But somehow it's hard to carry out your resolutions when irresistible temptations come. Still, I really will make an extra effort after this."

When the commonplace breakfast was over Diana appeared, crossing the white log bridge in the hollow, a gay little figure in her crimson ulster. Anne flew down the slope to meet her.

"Merry Christmas, Diana! And oh, it's a wonderful Christmas. I've something splendid to show you. Matthew has given me the loveliest dress, with such sleeves. I couldn't even imagine any nicer."

"I've got something more for you," said Diana breathlessly. "Here – this box. Aunt Josephine sent us out a big box with ever so many things in it – and this is for you. I'd have brought it over last night, but it didn't come until after dark, and I never feel very comfortable coming through the Haunted Wood in the dark now."

Anne opened the box and peeped in. First a card with "For the Anne-girl and Merry Christmas," written on it; and then, a pair of the daintiest little kid slippers, with beaded toes and satin bows and glistening buckles.

"Oh," said Anne, "Diana, this is too much. I must be dreaming."

"*I* call it providential," said Diana. "You won't have to borrow Ruby's slippers now, and that's a blessing, for they're two sizes too big for you, and it would be awful to hear a fairy shuffling. Josie Pye would be delighted. Mind you, Rob Wright went home with Gertie Pye from the practice night before last. Did you ever hear anything equal to that?"

All the Avonlea scholars were in a fever of excitement that day, for the hall had to be decorated and a last grand rehearsal held.

The concert came off in the evening and was a pronounced success. The little hall was crowded; all the performers did excellently well, but Anne was the bright particular star of the occasion, as even envy, in the shape of Josie Pye, dared not deny.

"Oh, hasn't it been a brilliant evening?" sighed Anne, when it was all over and she and Diana were walking home together under a dark, starry sky.

"Everything went off very well," said Diana practically. "I guess we must have made as much as ten dollars. Mind you, Mr Allan is going to send an account of it to the Charlottetown papers."

"Oh, Diana, will we really see our names in print? It makes me thrill to think of it. Your solo was perfectly elegant, Diana. I felt prouder than you did when it was encored. I just said to myself, 'It is my dear bosom friend who is so honoured.'"

"Well, your recitations just brought down the house, Anne. That sad one was simply splendid."

"Oh, I was so nervous, Diana. When Mr Allan called out my name I really cannot tell how I ever got up on that platform. I felt as if a million eyes were looking at me and through me, and for one dreadful moment I was sure I couldn't begin at all. Then I thought of my lovely puffed sleeves and took courage. I knew that I must live up to those sleeves, Diana. So I started in, and my voice seemed to be coming from ever so far away. I just felt like a parrot. It's providential that I practised those recitations so often up in the garret, or I'd never have been able to get through. Did I groan all right?"

"Yes, indeed, you groaned lovely," assured Diana.

"I saw old Mrs Sloane wiping away tears when I sat down. It was splendid to think I had touched somebody's heart. It's so romantic to take part in a concert, isn't it? Oh, it's been a very memorable occasion indeed."

"Wasn't the boys' dialogue fine?" said Diana. "Gilbert Blythe was just splendid. Anne, I do think it's awful mean the way you treat Gil. Wait till I tell you. When you ran off the platform after the fairy dialogue one of your roses fell out of your hair. I saw Gil pick it up and put it in his breast pocket. There now. You're so romantic that I'm sure you ought to be pleased at that."

"It's nothing to me what that person does," said Anne loftily. "I simply never waste a thought on him, Diana."

That night Marilla and Matthew, who had been out to a concert for the first time in twenty years, sat for a while by the kitchen fire after Anne had gone to bed.

"Well now, I guess our Anne did as well as any of them," said Matthew proudly.

"Yes, she did," admitted Marilla. "She's a bright child, Matthew. And she looked real nice too. I've been kind of opposed to this concert scheme, but I suppose there's no real harm in it after all. Anyhow, I was proud of Anne tonight, although I'm not going to tell her so."

"Well now, I was proud of her and I did tell her so 'fore she went upstairs," said Matthew. "We must see what we can do for her some of these days, Marilla. I guess she'll need something more than Avonlea school by and by."

"There's time enough to think of that," said Marilla. "She's only thirteen in March. Though tonight it struck me she was growing quite a big girl. Mrs Lynde made that dress a mite too long, and it makes Anne look so tall. She's quick to learn and I guess the best thing we can do for her will be to send her to Queen's after a spell. But nothing need be said about that for a year or two yet."

"Well now, it'll do no harm to be thinking it over off and on," said Matthew. "Things like that are all the better for lots of thinking over."

"Christmas Boxes"
from *What Katy Did at School*
by Susan Coolidge

Katy Carr is the hero of five books by Susan Coolidge. When we first meet her at the beginning of *What Katy Did*, she is a mischievous 12-year-old who likes to follow her own rules. But by the end of the book she has been forced to grow up quickly in order to help care for her family. So much so that when *What Katy Did at School* begins, her father decides it best to send her away to boarding school for a year so that she can have the chance of acting like a child again for a while. "I should like you to enjoy your youth while you have it," he says, "and not grow middle-aged before you are twenty."

Katy and her sister Clover have many adventures at Hilsover boarding school, and soon get into trouble with one of their strictest teachers, Miss Jane. But as the winter draws in, the girls face the prospect of their first Christmas away from their family. Luckily, they are about to receive a gift that is the next best thing to going home.

October was a delightful month, clear and sparkling; but early in November the weather changed, and became very cold. Thick frosts fell, every leaf vanished from the woods, in the gardens only blackened stalks remained to show where once the summer flowers had been. In spite of the stove outside the door, No. 2 began to be chilly; more than once Katy found her toothbrush stiff with ice in the morning. It was a foretaste of what the winter was to be, and the girls shivered at the prospect.

Toward the end of November Miss Jane caught a heavy cold. Unsparing of herself as of others, she went on hearing her classes as usual; and nobody paid much attention to her hoarseness and flushed cheeks, until she grew so much worse that she was forced to go to bed. There she stayed for nearly four weeks. It made a great change in the school; and the girls found it such a relief to have her sharp voice and eyes taken away that I am afraid they were rather glad of her illness than otherwise.

Katy shared in this feeling of relief. She did not like Miss Jane; it was pleasant not to have to see her or hear of her. But as day after day passed, and still she continued ill, Katy's conscience began to prick. One night she lay awake a long time, and heard Miss Jane coughing violently. Katy feared she was very sick, and wondered who took care of her all night and all day. None of the girls went near her. The servants were always busy. And Mrs Nipson, who did not love Miss Jane, was busy too.

In the morning, while studying and practising, Katy caught herself thinking over this question. At last she asked Miss Marsh:

"How is Miss Jane today?"

"About the same. She is not dangerously ill, the doctor says; but she coughs a great deal, and has some fever."

"Is anybody sitting with her?"

"Oh, no! there's no need of anyone. Susan answers the bell, and she has her medicine on the table within reach."

It sounded forlorn enough. Katy had lived in a sick-room so long herself that she knew just how dreary it is for an invalid to be left alone with "medicine within reach," and someone to answer a bell. She began to feel sorry for Miss Jane, and almost without intending it went down the entry, and tapped at her door. The "Come in!" sounded very faint; and Miss Jane as she lay in bed looked weak and dismal, and quite unlike the sharp, terrible person whom the girls feared so much. She was amazed at the sight of Katy, and made a feeble attempt to hold up her head and speak as usual.

"What is it, Miss Carr?"

"I only came to see how you are," said Katy, abashed at her own daring, "You coughed so much last night that I was afraid you were worse. Isn't there something I could do for you?"

"Thank you," said Miss Jane, "you are very kind." Think of Miss Jane's thanking anybody, and calling anybody kind!

"I should be very glad. Isn't there anything?" repeated Katy, encouraged.

"Well, I don't know: you might put another stick of wood on the fire," said Miss Jane, in an ungracious tone. Katy did so; and seeing that the iron cup on top of the stove was empty, she poured some water into it. Then she took a look about the room. Books and papers were scattered over the table; clean clothes from the wash lay on the chairs; nothing was in its place; and Katy, who knew how particular Miss Jane was on the subject of order, guessed at the discomfort which this untidy state of affairs must have caused her.

"Wouldn't you like to have me put these away?" she asked, touching the pile of clothes.

Miss Jane sighed impatiently, but she did not say no; so Katy, taking silence for consent, opened the drawers, and laid the clothes inside, guessing at the right places with a sort of instinct, and making as little noise and bustle as possible. Next she moved quietly to the table, where she sorted and arranged the papers, piled up the books, and put the pens and pencils in a small tray which stood there for the purpose. Lastly she began to dust the table with her pocket handkerchief, which proceeding roused Miss Jane at once.

"Don't," she said, "there is a duster in the cupboard."

Katy could not help smiling, but she found the duster, and proceeded to put the rest of the room into nice order, laying a fresh towel over the bedside table, and arranging watch, medicine, and spoon within reach. Miss Jane lay and watched her. I think she was as much surprised at herself for permitting all this, as Katy was at being permitted to do it. Sick people often consent because they feel too weak to object. After all, it *was* comfortable to have someone come in and straighten the things which for ten days past had vexed her neat eyes with their untidiness.

Lastly, smoothing the quilt, Katy asked if Miss Jane wouldn't like to have her pillow shaken up?

"I don't care," was the answer. It sounded discouraging; but Katy boldly seized the pillow, beat, smoothed, and put it again in place. Then she went out of the room as noiselessly as she could, Miss Jane never saying, "Thank you," or seeming to observe whether she went or stayed.

Rose Red and Clover could hardly believe their ears when told where she had been. They stared at her as people stare at Van Amburgh when he comes safely out of the lion's den.

"My stars!" exclaimed Rose, drawing a long breath. "You didn't really? And she hasn't bitten your head off!"

"Not a bit," said Katy, laughing. "What's more, I'm going again."

She was as good as her word. After that she went to see Miss Jane very often. Almost always there was some little thing which she could do, the fire needed mending, or the pitcher to be filled with ice-water, or

Miss Jane wanted the blinds opened or shut. Gradually she grew used to seeing Katy about the room. One morning she actually allowed her to brush her hair; and Katy's touch was so light and pleasant that afterwards Miss Jane begged her to do it every day.

"What makes you such a good nurse?" she asked one afternoon, rather abruptly.

"Being sick myself," replied Katy, gently. Then in answer to farther questioning, she told of her four years' illness, and her life upstairs, keeping house and studying lessons all alone by herself. Miss Jane did not say anything when she got through; but Katy fancied she looked at her in a new and kinder way.

So time went on till Christmas. It fell on a Friday that year, which shortened the holidays by a day, and disappointed many of the girls. Only a few went home, the rest were left to pass the time as best they might till Monday, when lessons were to begin again.

"It isn't much like merry Christmas," sighed Clover to herself, as she looked up at the uncottoned space at the top of the window, and saw great snowflakes wildly whirling by. No. 2 felt cold and dreary, and she was glad to exchange it for the school-room, round whose warm stove a cluster of girls was huddling. Everybody was in bad spirits; there was a tendency to talk about home, and the nice time which people were having there, and the very bad time they themselves were having at the Nunnery.

"Isn't it mis-e-ra-ble? I shall cry all night, I know I shall, I am so homesick," gulped Lilly, who had taken possession of her room-mate's shoulder and was weeping ostentatiously.

"I declare, you're just Mrs Gummidge in 'David Copperfield' over again," said Rose. "You recollect her, girls, don't you? When the porridge was burnt, you know – 'All of us felt the disappointment, but Mrs Gummidge felt it the most.' Isn't Lilly a real Mrs Gummidge, girls?"

The observation changed Lilly's tears into anger. "You're as hateful and as horrid as you can be, Rose Red," she exclaimed angrily. Then she flew out of the room, and shut the door behind her with a bang.

"There! she's gone upstairs to be mad," said Louisa Agnew.

"I don't care if she has," replied Rose, who was in a perverse mood.

"I wish you hadn't said that, Rosy," whispered Clover. "Lilly really felt badly."

"Well, what if she did? So do I feel badly, and you, and the rest of us. Lilly hasn't taken out a patent for bad feelings, which nobody must infringe. What business has she to make us feel badder, by setting up to be so much worse than the rest of the world?"

Clover said nothing, but went on with a book she was reading. In less than ten minutes, Rose, whose sun seldom stayed long behind a cloud, was at her elbow, dimpling and coaxing.

"I forgive you," she whispered, giving Clover's arm a little pinch.

"What for?"

"For being in the right. About Lilly, I mean. I was rather hateful to her, I confess. Never mind. When she comes downstairs, I'll make up. She's a crocodile, if ever there was one; but, as she's your cousin, I'll be good to her. Kiss me quick to prove that you're not vexed."

"Vexed indeed!" said Clover, kissing the middle of the pink cheek. "I wonder if anybody ever stayed vexed with you for ten minutes together, You Rosy-Posy you?"

"Bless you, yes! Miss Jane, for example. She hates me like poison, and all the time. Well, what of it? I know she's sick, but I 'can't tell a lie, pa,' on that account. Where's Katy?"

"Gone in to see her, I believe."

"One of these days," prophesied Rose, solemnly, "she'll go into that room, and she'll never come out again! Miss Jane is getting back into biting condition. I advise Katy to be careful. What's that noise? Sleigh-bells, I declare! Girls," – mounting a desk, and peeping out of the window – "somebody's got a big box – a big one! Here's old Joyce at the door, with his sledge. Now who do you suppose it is?"

"It's for me. I'm sure it's for me," cried half a dozen voices.

"Bella, my love, peep over the balusters, and see if you can't see the name," cried Louisa; and Bella, nothing loath, departed at once on this congenial errand.

"No, I can't," she reported, coming back from the hall. "The name's tipped up against the wall. There's two boxes! One is big, and one is little!"

"Oh, who can they be for?" clamored the girls. Half the school expected boxes, and had been watching the storm all day, with a dreadful fear that it would block the roads, and delay the expected treasures.

At this moment Mrs Nipson came in.

"There will be the usual study-hour this evening," she announced. "All of you will prepare lessons for

Monday morning. Miss Carr, come her for a moment, if you please."

Clover, wondering, followed her into the entry.

"A parcel has arrived for you, and a box," said Mrs Nipson. "I presume that they contain articles for Christmas. I will have the nails removed, and both of them placed in you room this evening, but I expect you to refrain from examining them until tomorrow. The vacation does not open until after study-hour tonight, and it will then be too late for you to begin."

"Very well, ma'am," said Clover, demurely. But the minute Mrs Nipson's back was turned, she gave a jump, and rushed into the school-room.

"O girls," she cried, "what do you think? Both the boxes are for Katy and me!"

"Both!" cried a disappointed chorus.

"Yes, both. Nipson said so. I'm so sorry for you. But isn't it nice for us? We've never had a box from home before, you know; and I didn't think we should, it's so far off. It's too lovely! But I do hope yours will come tonight."

Clover's voice was so sympathizing, for all its glee, that nobody could help being glad with her.

"You little darling!" said Louisa, giving her a hug. "I'm

rejoiced that the box is yours. The rest of us are always getting them, and you and Katy never had a thing before. I hope it's a nice one!"

Study-hour seemed unusually long that night. The minute it was over, the sisters ran to No. 2. There stood the boxes, a big wooden one, with all the nails taken out of the lid, and a small paper one, carefully tied up and sealed. It was almost more than the girls could do to obey orders and not peep.

"I feel something hard," announced Clover, inserting a finger-top under the lid.

"Oh, do you?" cried Katy. Then, making an heroic effort, she jumped into the bed.

"It's the only way," she said, "you'd better come too, Clovy. Blow the candle out and let's get to sleep as fast as we can, so as to make morning come quicker."

Katy dreamed of home that night. Perhaps it was that which made her wake so early. It was not five o'clock, and the room was perfectly dark. She did not like to disturb Clover, so she lay perfectly still, for hours as it seemed, till a faint gray dawn crept in, and revealed the outlines of the big box standing by the window. Then she could wait no longer, but crept out of bed, crossed the floor on tip-toe, and raising the lid a little put in her hand. Something crumby and sugary met it, and when she drew it out, there, fitting on her finger like a ring, was a round cake with a hole in the middle of it.

"Oh! it's one of Debby's jumbles!" she exclaimed.

"Where? What are you doing? Give me one too!" cried Clover, starting up. Katy rummaged till she found another, then, half frozen, she ran back to bed; and the two lay nibbling the jumbles, and talking about home, till dawn deepened into daylight, and morning was fairly come.

Breakfast was half an hour later than usual, which was comfortable. As soon as it was over, the girls proceeded to unpack their box. The day was so cold that they wrapped themselves in shawls, and Clover put on a hood and thick gloves. Rose Red, passing the door, burst out laughing, and recommended that she should add india rubbers and an umbrella.

"Come in," cried the sisters – "come in, and help us open our box."

"Oh, by the way, you have a box, haven't you?" said Rose, who was perfectly aware of the important fact, and had presented herself with the hope of being asked to look on. "Thank you, but perhaps I would better come some other time. I shall be in your way."

"You humbug!" said Clover, while Katy seized Rose and pulled her into the room. "There, sit on the bed, you ridiculous goose, and put on my gray cloak. How can you be so absurd as to say you won't? You know we want you, and you know you came on purpose!"

"Did I? Well, perhaps I did," laughed Rose. Then Katy lifted off the lid and set it against the door. It was an exciting moment.

"Just look here!" cried Katy.

The top of the box was mostly taken up with four square paper boxes, round which parcels of all shapes and sized were wedged and fitted. The whole was a miracle of packing. It had taken Miss Finch three mornings, with assistance from old Mary, and much advice from Elsie, to do it so beautifully.

Each box held a different kind of cake. One was of jumbles, another of ginger-snaps, a third of crullers, and the fourth contained a big square loaf of frosted plum-cake, with a circle of sugar almonds set in the frosting. How the trio exclaimed at this!

"I never imagined anything so nice," declared Rose, with her mouth full of jumble. "As for those snaps, they're simply perfect. What can be in all those fascinating bundles? Do hurry and open one, Katy."

Dear little Elsie! The first two bundles opened were hers, a white hood for Katy, and a blue one for Clover, both of her own knitting, and so nicely done. The girls were enchanted.

"How she has improved!" said Katy. "She knits better than either of us, Clover."

"There never was such a clever little darling!" responded Clover, and they patted the hoods, tried them on before the glass, and spent so much time in admiring them that Rose grew impatient.

"I declare," she cried, "it isn't any of my funeral, I know; but if you don't open another parcel soon, I shall certainly fall to myself. It seems as if, what with cold and curiosity, I couldn't wait."

"Very well," said Katy, laying aside her hood, with one final glance. "Take out a bundle, Clover. It's your turn."

Clover's bundle was for herself, "Evangeline," in blue and gold; and pretty soon "Golden Legend," in the same binding, appeared for Katy. Both these were from Dorry. Next came a couple of round packages of exactly the same size. These proved to be ink-stands, covered with Russia leather: one marked, "Katy from Johnnie," and the other, "Clover from Phil." It was evident that the children had done their shopping together, for presently two long narrow parcels revealed the carved pen-handles, precisely alike; and these were labelled, "Katy from Phil," and "Clover from Johnnie."

What fun it was opening those bundles! The girls made a long business of it, taking out but one at a time, exclaiming, admiring, and exhibiting to Rose, before they began upon another. They laughed, they joked, but I do not think it would have taken much to make either of them cry. It was almost too tender a pleasure, these proofs of loving remembrance from the little one; and each separate article seemed full of the very look and feel of home.

"What can this be?" said Katy, as she unrolled a paper and disclosed a pretty round box. She opened. Nothing was visible but pink cotton wool. Katy peeped beneath, and gave a cry.

"O Clovy! Such a lovely thing! It's from papa – of course it's from papa. How could he? It's a great deal too pretty."

The "lovely thing" was a long slender chain for Katy's watch, worked in fine yellow gold. Clover admired it extremely; and her joy knew no bounds when farther search revealed another box with a precisely similar chain for herself. It was too much. The girls fairly cried with pleasure.

"There never was such a papa in the world!" they said.

"Yes, there is. Mine is just as good," declared Rose, twinkling away a little tear-drop from her own eyes. "Now don't cry, honeys. Your papa's an angel, there's no doubt about it. I never saw such pretty chains in my life – never. As for the children, they're little ducks. You certainly are a wonderful family. Katy, I'm dying to know what is in the blue parcel."

The blue parcel was from Cecy, and contained a pretty blue ribbon for Clover. There was a pink one also, with a pink ribbon for Katy. Everybody had thought of the girls. Old Mary sent them each a yard measure; Miss Finch, a thread-case, stocked with differently coloured cottons. Alexander had cracked a bag full of hickory nuts.

"Did you ever?" said Rose, when this last was produced. "What a thing it is to be popular! Mrs Hall? Who's Mrs Hall?" as Clover unwrapped a tiny carved easel.

"She's Cecy's mother," explained Clover. "Wasn't she kind to send me this, Katy? And here's Cecy's photograph in a little frame for you."

Never was such a wonderful box. It appeared to have no bottom whatever. Under the presents were parcels of figs, prunes, almonds, raisins, candy; under those, apples and pears. There seemed no end to the surprises.

At last all were out.

"Now," said Katy, "let's throw back the apples and pears, and then I want you to help divide the other things, and make some packages for the girls. They are all disappointed not to have their boxes. I should like to have them share ours. Wouldn't you, Clover?"

"Yes, indeed. I was just going to propose it."

So Clover cut twenty-nine squares of white paper, Rose and Katy sorted and divided, and pretty soon ginger-snaps and almonds and sugar-plums were walking down all the entries, and a gladsome crunching showed that the girls had found pleasant employment. None of the snowed-up boxes got through till Monday, so except for Katy and Clover the school would have had no Christmas treat at all.

They carried Mrs Nipson a large slice of cake, and a basket full of the beautiful red apples. All the teachers were remembered, and the servants. The S. S. U. C. was convened and feasted; and as for Rose, Louisa, and other special cronies, dainties were heaped upon them with such unsparing hand that they finally remonstrated.

"You're giving everything away. You'll have none left for yourselves."

"Yes, we shall – plenty," said Clover. "O Rosy! here's such a splendid pear! You must have this."

"No! no!" protested Rose; but Clover forced it into her pocket. "The Carrs' Box" was always quoted in the Nunnery afterward, as an example of what papas and mammas could accomplish, when they were of the right sort, and really wanted to make school-girls happy. Distributing their treasures kept Katy and Clover so busy that it was not until after dinner that they found time to open the smaller box. When they did so, they were sorry for the delay. The box was full of flowers, roses, geranium-leaves, heliotrope, beautiful red and white carnations, all so bedded in cotton that the frost had not touched them. But they looked chilled, and Katy hastened to put them in warm water, which she had been told was the best way to revive drooping flowers.

Cousin Helen had sent them; and underneath, sewed to the box, that they might not shake about and do mischief, were two flat parcels wrapped in tissue paper, and tied with white ribbon, in Cousin Helen's, dainty way. They were glove-cases, of quilted silk, delicately scented, one white, and one lilac; and to each was pinned a loving note, wishing the girls a Merry Christmas.

"How awfully good people are!" said Clover. "I do think we ought to be the best girls in the world."

Last of all, Katy made a choice little selection from her stores, a splendid apple, a couple of fine pears, and handful of raisins and figs, and, with a few of the freshest flowers in a wine-glass, she went down the Row and tapped at Miss Jane's door.

Miss Jane was sitting up for the first time, wrapped in a shawl, and looking very thin and pale. Katy, who had almost ceased to be afraid of her, went in cheerily.

"We've had a delicious box from home, Miss Jane, full of all sorts of things. It has been such fun unpacking it! I've brought you an apple, some pears, and this little bunch of flowers. Wasn't it a nice Christmas for us?"

"Yes," said Miss Jane, "very nice indeed. I heard someone saying in the entry that you had a box. Thank you," as Katy set the basket and glass on the table. "Those flowers are very sweet. I wish you a Merry Christmas, I'm sure."

This was much from Miss Jane, who couldn't help

speaking shortly, even when she was pleased. Katy withdrew in high glee.

But that night, just before bed-time, something happened so surprising that Katy, telling Clover of it afterward, said she half fancied that she must have dreamed it all. It was about eight o'clock in the evening: she was passing down Quaker Row, and Miss Jane called and asked her to come in. Miss Jane's cheeks were flushed, and she spoke fast, as if she had resolved to say something, and thought the sooner it was over the better.

"Miss Carr," she began, "I wish to tell you that I made up my mind some time since that we did you an injustice last term. It is not your attentions to me during my illness which have changed my opinion – that was done before I fell ill. It is your general conduct, and the good influence which I have seen you exert over other girls, which convinced me that we must have been wrong about you. That is all. I thought you might like to hear me say this, and I shall say the same to Mrs Nipson."

"Thank you," said Katy, "you don't know how glad I am!" She half thought she would kiss Miss Jane, but somehow it didn't seem possible; so she shook hands very heartily instead, and flew to her room, feeling as if her feet were wings.

"It seems too good to be true. I want to cry, I am so happy," she told Clover. "What a lovely day this has been!"

And of all that she had received, I think Katy considered this explanation with Miss Jane as her very best Christmas box.

"The First Journey with the Reindeer"
From *The Life and Adventures of Santa Claus*
by L. Frank Baum

There have been countless stories, poems and songs written about Santa Claus, and perhaps this is because there are so many unanswered questions about the man. Where did he come from? Why does he deliver presents? And how can he visit all the children of the world in just one night?

These questions have fired the imaginations of writers for many years. One of the earliest to try and answer some of them was *Wizard of Oz* author L. Frank Baum in his book *The Life and Adventures of Santa Claus*.

The story provides many interesting answers to some of these questions. It tells of how Santa was abandoned as an infant in the Forest of Burzee and raised by the lioness Shiegra, and that he first became a toymaker after making a carving of his cat, Blinky.

The following chapter tells a familiar part of the Santa story – how he first met the reindeer and convinced them to carry him around the world to deliver his toys.

Those were happy days for Claus when he carried his accumulation of toys to the children who had awaited them so long. During his imprisonment in the Valley he had been so industrious that all his shelves were filled with playthings, and after quickly supplying the little ones living near by he saw he must now extend his travels to wider fields.

Remembering the time when he had journeyed with Ak through all the world, he knew children were everywhere, and he longed to make as many as possible happy with his gifts.

So he loaded a great sack with all kinds of toys, slung it upon his back that he might carry it more easily, and started off on a longer trip than he had yet undertaken.

Wherever he showed his merry face, in hamlet or in farmhouse, he received a cordial welcome, for his fame had spread into far lands. At each village the children swarmed about him, following his footsteps wherever he went; and the women thanked him gratefully for the joy he brought their little ones; and the men looked upon him curiously that he should devote his time to such a queer occupation as toy-making. But everyone smiled on him and gave him kindly words, and Claus felt amply repaid for his long journey.

When the sack was empty he went back again to the Laughing Valley and once more filled it to the brim. This time he followed another road, into a different part of the country, and carried happiness to many children who never before had owned a toy or guessed that such a delightful plaything existed.

After a third journey, so far away that Claus was many days walking the distance, the store of toys became exhausted and without delay he set about making a fresh supply.

From seeing so many children and studying their tastes he had acquired several new ideas about toys.

The dollies were, he had found, the most delightful of all playthings for babies and little girls, and often those who could not say "dolly" would call for a "doll" in their sweet baby talk. So Claus resolved to make many dolls, of all sizes, and to dress them in bright-coloured clothing. The older boys – and even some of the girls – loved the images of animals, so he still made cats and elephants and horses. And many of the little fellows had musical natures, and longed for drums and cymbals and whistles and horns. So he made a number of toy drums, with tiny sticks to beat them with; and he made whistles from the willow trees, and horns from the bog-reeds, and cymbals from bits of beaten metal.

All this kept him busily at work, and before he realized it the winter season came, with deeper snows than usual, and he knew he could not leave the Valley with his heavy pack. Moreover, the next trip would take him farther from home than every before, and Jack Frost was mischievous enough to nip his nose and ears if he undertook the long journey while the Frost King reigned. The Frost King was Jack's father and never reproved him for his pranks.

So Claus remained at his work-bench; but he whistled and sang as merrily as ever, for he would allow no disappointment to sour his temper or make him unhappy.

One bright morning he looked from his window and saw two of the deer he had known in the Forest walking toward his house.

Claus was surprised; not that the friendly deer should visit him, but that they walked on the surface of the snow as easily as if it were solid ground, notwithstanding the fact that throughout the Valley the snow lay many feet deep. He had walked out of his house a day or two before and had sunk to his armpits in a drift.

So when the deer came near he opened the door and called to them:

"Good morning, Flossie! Tell me how you are able to walk on the snow so easily."

"It is frozen hard," answered Flossie.

"The Frost King has breathed on it," said Glossie, coming up, "and the surface is now as solid as ice."

"Perhaps," remarked Claus, thoughtfully, "I might now carry my pack of toys to the children."

"Is it a long journey?" asked Flossie.

"Yes; it will take me many days, for the pack is heavy," answered Claus.

"Then the snow would melt before you could get back," said the deer. "You must wait until spring, Claus."

Claus sighed. "Had I your fleet feet," said he, "I could make the journey in a day."

"But you have not," returned Glossie, looking at his

own slender legs with pride.

"Perhaps I could ride upon your back," Claus ventured to remark, after a pause.

"Oh no; our backs are not strong enough to bear your weight," said Flossie, decidedly. "But if you had a sledge, and could harness us to it, we might draw you easily, and your pack as well."

"I'll make a sledge!" exclaimed Claus. "Will you agree to draw me if I do?"

"Well," replied Flossie, "we must first go and ask the Knooks, who are our guardians, for permission; but if they consent, and you can make a sledge and harness, we will gladly assist you."

"Then go at once!" cried Claus, eagerly. "I am sure the friendly Knooks will give their consent, and by the time you are back I shall be ready to harness you to my sledge."

Flossie and Glossie, being deer of much intelligence, had long wished to see the great world, so they gladly ran over the frozen snow to ask the Knooks if they might carry Claus on his journey.

Meantime the toy-maker hurriedly began the construction of a sledge, using material from his wood-pile. He made two long runners that turned upward at the front ends, and across these nailed short boards, to make a platform. It was soon completed, but was as rude in appearance as it is possible for a sledge to be.

The harness was more difficult to prepare, but Claus twisted strong cords together and knotted them so they would fit around the necks of the deer, in the shape of a collar. From these ran other cords to fasten the deer to the front of the sledge.

Before the work was completed Glossie and Flossie were back from the Forest, having been granted permission by Will Knook to make the journey with Claus provided they would to Burzee by daybreak the next morning.

"That is not a very long time," said Flossie; "but we are swift and strong, and if we get started by this evening we can travel many miles during the night."

Claus decided to make the attempt, so he hurried on his preparations as fast as possible. After a time he fastened the collars around the necks of his steeds and harnessed them to his rude sledge. Then he placed a stool on the little platform, to serve as a seat, and filled a sack with his prettiest toys.

"How do you intend to guide us?" asked Glossie. "We have never been out of the Forest before, except to visit your house, so we shall not know the way."

Claus thought about that for a moment. Then he brought more cords and fastened two of them to the spreading antlers of each deer, one on the right and the other on the left.

"Those will be my reins," said Claus, "and when I pull them to the right or to the left you must go in that direction. If I do not pull the reins at all you may go straight ahead."

"Very well," answered Glossie and Flossie; and then they asked: "Are you ready?"

Claus seated himself upon the stool, placed the sack of toys at his feet, and then gathered up the reins.

"All ready!" he shouted; "away we go!"

The deer leaned forward, lifted their slender limbs, and the next moment away flew the sledge over the frozen snow. The swiftness of the motion surprised Claus, for in a few strides they were across the Valley and gliding over the broad plain beyond.

The day had melted into evening by the time they started; for, swiftly as Claus had worked, many hours had been consumed in making his preparations. But the moon shone brightly to light their way, and Claus soon decided it was just as pleasant to travel by night as by day.

The deer liked it better; for, although they wished to see something of the world, they were timid about meeting men, and now all the dwellers in the towns and farmhouses were sound asleep and could not see them.

Away and away they sped, on and on over the hills and through the valleys and across the plains until they reached a village where Claus had never been before.

Here he called on them to stop, and they immediately obeyed. But a new difficulty now presented itself, for the people had locked their doors when they went to bed, and Claus found he could not enter the houses to leave his toys.

"I am afraid, my friends, we have made our journey for nothing," said he, "for I shall be obliged to carry my playthings back home again without giving them to the children of this village."

"What's the matter?" asked Flossie.

"The doors are locked," answered Claus, "and I can not get in."

Glossie looked around at the houses. The snow was quite deep in that village, and just before them was a roof only a few feet above the sledge. A broad chimney, which seemed to Glossie big enough to admit Claus, was at the peak of the roof.

"Why don't you climb down that chimney?" asked Glossie.

Claus looked at it.

"That would be easy enough if I were on top of the roof," he answered.

"Then hold fast and we will take you there," said the deer, and they gave one bound to the roof and landed beside the big chimney.

"Good!" cried Claus, well pleased, and he slung the pack of toys over his shoulder and got into the chimney.

There was plenty of soot on the bricks, but he did not mind that, and by placing his hands and knees against the sides he crept downward until he had reached the fireplace. Leaping lightly over the smoldering coals he found himself in a large sitting-room, where a dim light was burning.

From this room two doorways led into smaller chambers. In one a woman lay asleep, with a baby beside her in a crib.

Claus laughed, but he did not laugh aloud for fear of waking the baby. Then he slipped a big doll from his pack and laid it in the crib. The little one smiled, as if it dreamed of the pretty plaything it was to find on the morrow, and Claus crept softly from the room and entered at the other doorway.

Here were two boys, fast asleep with their arms around each other's neck. Claus gazed at them lovingly a moment and then placed upon the bed a drum, two horns and a wooden elephant.

He did not linger, now that his work in this house was done, but climbed the chimney again and seated himself on his sledge.

"Can you find another chimney?" he asked the reindeer.

"Easily enough," replied Glossie and Flossie.

Down to the edge of the roof they raced, and then, without pausing, leaped through the air to the top of the next building, where a huge, old-fashioned chimney stood.

"Don't be so long, this time," called Flossie, "or we shall never get back to the Forest by daybreak."

Claus made a trip down this chimney also and found five children sleeping in the house, all of whom were quickly supplied with toys.

When he returned the deer sprang to the next roof, but on descending the chimney Claus found no children there at all. That was not often the case in this village, however, so he lost less time than you might suppose in visiting the dreary homes where there were no little ones.

When he had climbed down the chimneys of all the houses in that village, and had left a toy for every sleeping child, Claus found that his great sack was not yet half emptied.

"Onward, friends!" he called to the deer; "we must seek another village."

So away they dashed, although it was long past midnight, and in a surprisingly short time they came to a large city, the largest Claus had ever visited since he began to make toys. But, nothing daunted by the throng of houses, he set to work at once and his beautiful steeds carried him rapidly from one roof to another, only the highest being beyond the leaps of the agile deer.

At last the supply of toys was exhausted and Claus seated himself in the sledge, with the empty sack at his feet, and turned the heads of Glossie and Flossie toward home.

Presently Flossie asked:

"What is that gray streak in the sky?"

"It is the coming dawn of day," answered Claus,

surprised to find that it was so late.

"Good gracious!" exclaimed Glossie; "then we shall not be home by daybreak, and the Knooks will punish us and never let us come again."

"We must race for the Laughing Valley and make our best speed," returned Flossie; "so hold fast, friend Claus!"

Claus held fast and the next moment was flying so swiftly over the snow that he could not see the trees as they whirled past. Up hill and down dale, swift as an arrow shot from a bow they dashed, and Claus shut his eyes to keep the wind out of them and left the deer to find their own way.

It seemed to him they were plunging through space, but he was not at all afraid. The Knooks were severe masters, and must be obeyed at all hazards, and the gray streak in the sky was growing brighter every moment.

Finally the sledge came to a sudden stop and Claus, who was taken unawares, tumbled from his seat into a snowdrift. As he picked himself up he heard the deer crying:

"Quick, friend, quick! Cut away our harness!"

He drew his knife and rapidly severed the cords, and then he wiped the moisture from his eyes and looked around him.

The sledge had come to a stop in the Laughing Valley, only a few feet, he found, from his own door. In the East the day was breaking, and turning to the edge of Burzee he saw Glossie and Flossie just disappearing in the Forest.

Santa Claus!

Claus thought that none of the children would ever know where the toys came from which they found by their bedsides when they wakened the following morning. But kindly deeds are sure to bring fame, and fame has many wings to carry its tidings into far lands; so for miles and miles in every direction people were talking of Claus and his wonderful gifts to children. The sweet generousness of his work caused a few selfish folk to sneer, but even these were forced to admit their respect for a man so gentle-natured that he loved to devote his life to pleasing the helpless little ones of his race.

Therefore the inhabitants of every city and village had been eagerly watching the coming of Claus, and remarkable stories of his beautiful playthings were told the children to keep them patient and contented.

When, on the morning following the first trip of Claus with his deer, the little ones came running to their parents with the pretty toys they had found, and asked from whence they came, they was but one reply to the question.

"The good Claus must have been here, my darlings; for his are the only toys in all the world!"

"But how did he get in?" asked the children.

At this the fathers shook their heads, being themselves unable to understand how Claus had gained admittance to their homes; but the mothers, watching the glad faces of their dear ones, whispered that the good Claus was no mortal man but assuredly a Saint, and they piously blessed his name for the happiness he had bestowed upon their children.

"A Saint," said one, with bowed head, "has no need to unlock doors if it pleases him to enter our homes."

And, afterward, when a child was naughty or disobedient, its mother would say:

"You must pray to the good Santa Claus for forgiveness. He does not like naughty children, and, unless you repent, he will bring you no more pretty toys."

But Santa Claus himself would not have approved

this speech. He brought toys to the children because they were little and helpless, and because he loved them. He knew that the best of children were sometimes naughty, and that the naughty ones were often good. It is the way with children, the world over, and he would not have changed their natures had he possessed the power to do so.

And that is how our Claus became Santa Claus. It is possible for any man, by good deeds, to enshrine himself as a Saint in the hearts of the people.

"Christmas Storms and Sunshine"
by Elizabeth Gaskell

Elizabeth Gaskell is best known for works such as *Cranford* and *North and South*, but before she published her first novel, she published several short stories under the pseudonym "Cotton Mather Mills", including the following Christmas story.

It's a tale of two neighbouring families with two very different visions of what Christmas should be – the Jenkinses, who want to splash out on a lavish feast, and the Hodgsons who want a simple and humble meal.

In the town of —— (no matter where) there circulated two local newspapers (no matter when). Now the *Flying Post* was long established and respectable – alias bigoted and Tory; the *Examiner* was spirited and intelligent – alias new-fangled and democratic. Every week these newspapers contained articles abusing each other; as cross and peppery as articles could be, and evidently the production of irritated minds, although they seemed to have one stereotyped commencement – "Though the article appearing in last week's *Post* (or *Examiner*) is below contempt, yet we have been induced," &c., &c., and every Saturday the Radical shopkeepers shook hands together, and agreed that the *Post* was done for, by the slashing, clever *Examiner*; while the more dignified Tories began by regretting that Johnson should think that low paper, only read by a few of the vulgar, worth wasting his wit upon; however the *Examiner* was at its last gasp.

It was not though. It lived and flourished; at least it paid its way, as one of the heroes of my story could tell. He was chief compositor, or whatever title may be given to the head-man of the mechanical part of a newspaper. He hardly confined himself to that department. Once or twice, unknown to the editor, when the manuscript had fallen short, he had filled up the vacant space by compositions of his own; announcements of a forthcoming crop of green peas in December; a grey thrush having been seen, or a white hare, or such interesting phenomena; invented for the occasion, I must confess; but what of that? His wife always knew when to expect a little specimen of her husband's literary talent by a peculiar cough, which served as prelude; and, judging from this encouraging sign, and the high-pitched and emphatic voice in which he read them, she was inclined to think, that an "Ode to an early Rose-bud," in the corner devoted to original poetry, and a letter in the correspondence department, signed "Pro Bono Publico," were her husband's writing, and to hold up her head accordingly.

I never could find out what it was that occasioned the

Hodgsons to lodge in the same house as the Jenkinses. Jenkins held the same office in the Tory paper as Hodgson did in the *Examiner*, and, as I said before, I leave you to give it a name. But Jenkins had a proper sense of his position, and a proper reverence for all in authority, from the king down to the editor and sub-editor. He would as soon have thought of borrowing the king's crown for a nightcap, or the king's sceptre for a walking-stick, as he would have thought of filling up any spare corner with any production of his own; and I think it would have even added to his contempt of Hodgson (if that were possible), had he known of the "productions of his brain," as the latter fondly alluded to the paragraphs he inserted, when speaking to his wife.

Jenkins had his wife too. Wives were wanting to finish the completeness of the quarrel, which existed one memorable Christmas week, some dozen years ago, between the two neighbours, the two compositors. And with wives, it was a very pretty, a very complete quarrel. To make the opposing parties still more equal, still more well-matched, if the Hodgsons had a baby ("such a baby! – a poor, puny little thing"), Mrs Jenkins had a cat ("such a cat! a great, nasty, miowling tom-cat, that was always stealing the milk put by for little Angel's supper"). And now, having matched Greek with Greek, I must proceed to the tug of war. It was the day before Christmas; such a cold east wind! such an inky sky! such a blue-black look in people's faces, as they were driven out more than usual, to complete their purchases for the next day's festival.

Before leaving home that morning, Jenkins had given some money to his wife to buy the next day's dinner.

"My dear, I wish for turkey and sausages. It may be a weakness, but I own I am partial to sausages. My deceased mother was. Such tastes are hereditary. As to the sweets – whether plum-pudding or mince-pies – I leave such considerations to you; I only beg you not to mind expense. Christmas comes but once a year."

And again he had called out from the bottom of the first flight of stairs, just close to the Hodgsons' door ("such ostentatiousness," as Mrs Hodgson observed), "You will not forget the sausages, my dear?"

"I should have liked to have had something above common, Mary," said Hodgson, as they too made their plans for the next day, "but I think roast beef must do for us. You see, love, we've a family."

"Only one, Jem! I don't want more than roast beef,

though, I'm sure. Before I went to service, mother and me would have thought roast beef a very fine dinner."

"Well, let's settle it then, roast beef and a plum-pudding; and now, goodbye. Mind and take care of little Tom. I thought he was a bit hoarse this morning."

And off he went to his work.

Now, it was a good while since Mrs Jenkins and Mrs Hodgson had spoken to each other, although they were quite as much in possession of the knowledge of events and opinions as though they did. Mary knew that Mrs Jenkins despised her for not having a real lace cap, which Mrs Jenkins had; and for having been a servant, which Mrs Jenkins had not; and the little occasional pinchings which the Hodgsons were obliged to resort to, to make both ends meet, would have been very patiently endured by Mary, if she had not winced under Mrs Jenkins's knowledge of such economy. But she had her revenge. She had a child, and Mrs Jenkins had none. To have had a child, even such a puny baby as little Tom, Mrs Jenkins would have worn commonest caps, and cleaned grates, and drudged her fingers to the bone. The great unspoken disappointment of her life soured her temper, and turned her thoughts inward, and made her morbid and selfish.

"Hang that cat! he's been stealing again! he's gnawed the cold mutton in his nasty mouth till it's not fit to set before a Christian; and I've nothing else for Jem's dinner. But I'll give it him now I've caught him, that I will!"

So saying, Mary Hodgson caught up her husband's Sunday cane, and despite pussy's cries and scratches, she gave him such a beating as she hoped might cure him of his thievish propensities; when lo! and behold, Mrs Jenkins stood at the door with a face of bitter wrath.

"Aren't you ashamed of yourself, ma'am, to abuse a poor dumb animal, ma'am, as knows no better than to take food when he sees it, ma'am? He only follows the nature which God has given, ma'am; and it's a pity your nature, ma'am, which I've heard, is of the stingy saving species, does not make you shut your cupboard-door a little closer. There is such a thing as law for brute animals. I'll ask Mr Jenkins, but I don't think them Radicals has done away with that law yet, for all their Reform Bill, ma'am. My poor precious love of a Tommy, is he hurt? and is his leg broke for taking a mouthful of scraps, as most people would give away to a beggar – if he'd take 'em?" wound up Mrs Jenkins, casting a contemptuous look on the remnant of a scrag end of mutton.

Mary felt very angry and very guilty. For she really pitied the poor limping animal as he crept up to his mistress, and there lay down to bemoan himself; she wished she had not beaten him so hard, for it certainly was her own careless way of never shutting the cupboard-door that had tempted him to his fault. But the sneer at her little bit of mutton turned her penitence to fresh wrath, and she shut the door in Mrs Jenkins's face, as she stood caressing her cat in the lobby, with such a bang, that it wakened little Tom, and he began to cry.

Everything was to go wrong with Mary today. Now baby was awake, who was to take her husband's dinner to the office? She took the child in her arms, and tried to hush him off to sleep again, and as she sung she cried, she could hardly tell why – a sort of reaction from her violent angry feelings. She wished she had never beaten the poor cat; she wondered if his leg was really broken. What would her mother say if she knew how cross and cruel her little Mary was getting? If she should live to beat her child in one of her angry fits?

It was of no use lullabying while she sobbed so; it must be given up, and she must just carry her baby in her arms, and take him with her to the office, for it was long past dinner-time. So she pared the mutton carefully, although by so doing she reduced the meat to an infinitesimal quantity, and taking the baked potatoes out of the oven, she popped them piping hot into her basket with the et-ceteras of plate, butter, salt, and knife and fork.

It was, indeed, a bitter wind. She bent against it as she ran, and the flakes of snow were sharp and cutting as ice. Baby cried all the way, though she cuddled him up in her shawl. Then her husband had made his appetite up for a potato pie, and (literary man as he was) his body got so much the better of his mind, that he looked rather black at the cold mutton. Mary had no appetite for her own dinner when she arrived at home again. So, after she had tried to feed baby, and he had fretfully refused to take his bread and milk, she laid him down as usual on his quilt, surrounded by playthings, while she sided away, and chopped suet for the next day's pudding. Early in the afternoon a parcel came, done up first in brown paper, then in such a white, grass-bleached, sweet-smelling towel, and a note from her dear, dear mother; in which quaint writing she endeavoured to tell her daughter that she was not forgotten at Christmas time; but that learning that Farmer Burton was killing his pig, she had made interest for some of his famous pork, out of which she had manufactured some sausages, and flavoured them just as Mary used to like when she lived at home.

"Dear, dear mother!" said Mary to herself. "There never was anyone like her for remembering other folk. What rare sausages she used to make! Home things have a smack with 'em, no bought things can ever have. Set them up with their sausages! I've a notion if Mrs Jenkins had ever tasted mother's she'd have no fancy for them town-made things Fanny took in just now."

And so she went on thinking about home, till the smiles and the dimples came out again at the remembrance of that pretty cottage, which would look green even now in the depth of winter, with its pyracanthus, and its holly-bushes, and the great Portugal laurel that was her mother's pride. And the back path through the orchard to Farmer Burton's; how well she remembered it. The bushels of unripe apples she had picked up there, and distributed among his pigs, till he had scolded her for giving them so much green trash.

She was interrupted – her baby (I call him a baby, because his father and mother did, and because he was so little of his age, but I rather think he was eighteen months old,) had fallen asleep some time before among his playthings; an uneasy, restless sleep; but of which Mary had been thankful, as his morning's nap had been too short, and as she was so busy. But now he began to make such a strange crowing noise, just like a chair drawn heavily and gratingly along a kitchen-floor! His eyes were open, but expressive of nothing but pain.

"Mother's darling!" said Mary, in terror, lifting him up. "Baby, try not to make that noise. Hush, hush, darling; what hurts him?" But the noise came worse and worse.

"Fanny! Fanny!" Mary called in mortal fright, for her baby was almost black with his gasping breath, and she had no one to ask for aid or sympathy but her landlady's daughter, a little girl of twelve or thirteen, who attended to the house in her mother's absence, as daily cook in gentlemen's families. Fanny was more especially considered the attendant of the upstairs lodgers (who paid for the use of the kitchen, "for Jenkins could not abide the smell of meat cooking"), but just now she was fortunately sitting at her afternoon's work of darning stockings, and hearing Mrs Hodgson's cry of terror, she ran to her sitting-room, and understood the case at a glance.

"He's got the croup! Oh, Mrs Hodgson, he'll die as

sure as fate. Little brother had it, and he died in no time. The doctor said he could do nothing for him – it had gone too far. He said if we'd put him in a warm bath at first, it might have saved him; but, bless you! he was never half so bad as your baby." Unconsciously there mingled in her statement some of a child's love of producing an effect; but the increasing danger was clear enough.

"Oh, my baby! my baby! Oh, love, love! don't look so ill; I cannot bear it. And my fire so low! There, I was thinking of home, and picking currants, and never minding the fire. Oh, Fanny! what is the fire like in the kitchen? Speak."

"Mother told me to screw it up, and throw some slack on as soon as Mrs Jenkins had done with it, and so I did. It's very low and black. But, oh, Mrs Hodgson! let me run for the doctor – I cannot abear to hear him, it's so like little brother."

Through her streaming tears Mary motioned her to go; and trembling, sinking, sick at heart, she laid her boy in his cradle, and ran to fill her kettle.

Mrs Jenkins, having cooked her husband's snug little dinner, to which he came home; having told him her story of pussy's beating, at which he was justly and dignifiedly indignant, saying it was all of a piece with that abusive *Examiner*; having received the sausages, and turkey, and mince pies, which her husband had ordered; and cleaned up the room, and prepared everything for tea, and coaxed and duly bemoaned her cat (who had pretty nearly forgotten his beating, but very much enjoyed the petting), having done all these and many other things, Mrs Jenkins sate down to get up the real lace cap. Every thread was pulled out separately, and carefully stretched: when, what was that? Outside, in the street, a chorus of piping children's voices sang the old carol she had heard a hundred times in the days of her youth:

> "As Joseph was a walking he heard an
>   angel sing,
> 'This night shall be born our heavenly
>   King.
> He neither shall be born in housen nor in
>   hall,
> Nor in the place of Paradise, but in an ox's
>   stall.
> He neither shall be clothed in purple nor
>   in pall,
> But all in fair linen, as were babies all:

He neither shall be rocked in silver nor in
    gold,
But in a wooden cradle that rocks on the
    mould,'" &c.

She got up and went to the window. There, below, stood the group of grey black little figures, relieved against the snow, which now enveloped everything. "For old sake's sake," as she phrased it, she counted out a halfpenny apiece for the singers, out of the copper bag, and threw them down below.

The room had become chilly while she had been counting out and throwing down her money, so she stirred her already glowing fire, and sat down right before it – but not to stretch her lace; like Mary Hodgson, she began to think over long-past days, on softening remembrances of the dead and gone, on words long forgotten, on holy stories heard at her mother's knee.

"I cannot think what's come over me tonight," said she, half aloud, recovering herself by the sound of her own voice from her train of thought – "My head goes wandering on them old times. I'm sure more texts have come into my head with thinking on my mother within this last half hour, than I've thought on for years and years. I hope I'm not going to die. Folks say, thinking too much on the dead betokens we're going to join 'em; I should be loth to go just yet – such a fine turkey as we've got for dinner tomorrow, too!"

Knock, knock, knock, at the door, as fast as knuckles could go. And then, as if the comer could not wait, the door was opened, and Mary Hodgson stood there as white as death.

"Mrs Jenkins! – oh, your kettle is boiling, thank God! Let me have the water for my baby, for the love of God! He's got croup, and is dying!"

Mrs Jenkins turned on her chair with a wooden inflexible look on her face, that (between ourselves) her husband knew and dreaded for all his pompous dignity.

"I'm sorry I can't oblige you, ma'am; my kettle is wanted for my husband's tea. Don't be afeared, Tommy, Mrs Hodgson won't venture to intrude herself where she's not desired. You'd better send for the doctor, ma'am, instead of wasting your time in wringing your hands, ma'am – my kettle is engaged."

Mary clasped her hands together with passionate force, but spoke no word of entreaty to that wooden face – that sharp, determined voice; but, as she turned away, she prayed for strength to bear the coming trial, and strength to forgive Mrs Jenkins.

Mrs Jenkins watched her go away meekly, as one who has no hope, and then she turned upon herself as sharply as she ever did on anyone else.

"What a brute I am, Lord forgive me! What's my husband's tea to a baby's life? In croup, too, where time is everything. You crabbed old vixen, you! – anyone may know you never had a child!"

She was downstairs (kettle in hand) before she had finished her self-upbraiding; and when in Mrs Hodgson's room, she rejected all thanks (Mary had not the voice for many words), saying, stiffly, "I do it for the poor babby's sake, ma'am, hoping he may live to have mercy to poor dumb beasts, if he does forget to lock his cupboards."

But she did everything, and more than Mary, with her young inexperience, could have thought of. She prepared the warm bath, and tried it with her husband's own thermometer (Mr Jenkins was as punctual as clockwork in noting down the temperature of every day). She let his mother place her baby in the tub, still preserving the same rigid, affronted aspect, and then she went upstairs without a word. Mary longed to ask her to stay, but dared not; though, when she left the room, the tears chased each other down her cheeks faster than ever. Poor young mother! how she counted the minutes till the doctor should come. But, before he came, down again stalked Mrs Jenkins, with something in her hand.

"I've seen many of these croup-fits, which, I take it, you've not, ma'am. Mustard plaisters is very sovereign, put on the throat; I've been up and made one, ma'am, and, by your leave, I'll put it on the poor little fellow."

Mary could not speak, but she signed her grateful assent.

It began to smart while they still kept silence; and he looked up to his mother as if seeking courage from her looks to bear the stinging pain; but she was softly crying, to see him suffer, and her want of courage reacted upon him, and he began to sob aloud. Instantly Mrs Jenkins's apron was up, hiding her face: "Peep-bo, baby," said she, as merrily as she could. His little face brightened, and his mother having once got the cue, the two women kept the little fellow amused, until his plaister had taken effect.

"He's better – oh, Mrs Jenkins, look at his eyes! how different! And he breathes quite softly—"

As Mary spoke thus, the doctor entered. He examined his patient. Baby was really better.

"It has been a sharp attack, but the remedies you have applied have been worth all the Pharmacopœia an hour later. – I shall send a powder," &c. &c.

Mrs Jenkins stayed to hear this opinion; and (her heart wonderfully more easy) was going to leave the room, when Mary seized her hand and kissed it; she could not speak her gratitude.

Mrs Jenkins looked affronted and awkward, and as if she must go upstairs and wash her hand directly.

But, in spite of these sour looks, she came softly down an hour or so afterwards to see how baby was.

The little gentleman slept well after the fright he had given his friends; and on Christmas morning, when Mary awoke and looked at the sweet little pale face lying on her arm, she could hardly realize the danger he had been in.

When she came down (later than usual), she found the household in a commotion. What do you think had happened? Why, pussy had been a traitor to his best friend, and eaten up some of Mr Jenkins's own especial sausages; and gnawed and tumbled the rest so, that they were not fit to be eaten! There were no bounds to that cat's appetite! he would have eaten his own father if he had been tender enough. And now Mrs Jenkins stormed and cried – "Hang the cat!"

Christmas Day, too! and all the shops shut! "What was turkey without sausages?" gruffly asked Mr Jenkins.

"Oh, Jem!" whispered Mary, "hearken what a piece of work he's making about sausages – I should like to take Mrs Jenkins up some of mother's; they're twice as good as bought sausages."

"I see no objection, my dear. Sausages do not involve intimacies, else his politics are what I can no ways respect."

"But, oh, Jem, if you had seen her last night about baby! I'm sure she may scold me for ever, and I'll not answer. I'd even make her cat welcome to the sausages." The tears gathered to Mary's eyes as she kissed her boy.

"Better take 'em upstairs, my dear, and give them to the cat's mistress." And Jem chuckled at his saying.

Mary put them on a plate, but still she loitered.

"What must I say, Jem? I never know."

"Say – I hope you'll accept of these sausages, as my mother – no, that's not grammar; – say what comes uppermost, Mary, it will be sure to be right."

So Mary carried them upstairs and knocked at the door; and when told to "come in," she looked very red, but went up to Mrs Jenkins, saying, "Please take these.

Mother made them." And was away before an answer could be given.

Just as Hodgson was ready to go to church, Mrs Jenkins came downstairs, and called Fanny. In a minute, the latter entered the Hodgsons' room, and delivered Mr and Mrs Jenkins's compliments, and they would be particular glad if Mr and Mrs Hodgson would eat their dinner with them.

"And carry baby upstairs in a shawl, be sure," added Mrs Jenkins's voice in the passage, close to the door, whither she had followed her messenger. There was no discussing the matter, with the certainty of every word being overheard.

Mary looked anxiously at her husband. She remembered his saying he did not approve of Mr Jenkins's politics.

"Do you think it would do for baby?" asked he.

"Oh, yes," answered she, eagerly; "I would wrap him up so warm."

"And I've got our room up to sixty-five already, for all it's so frosty," added the voice outside.

Now, how do you think they settled the matter? The very best way in the world. Mr and Mrs Jenkins came down into the Hodgsons' room, and dined there. Turkey at the top, roast beef at the bottom, sausages at one side, potatoes at the other. Second course, plum-pudding at the top, and mince pies at the bottom.

And after dinner, Mrs Jenkins would have baby on her knee; and he seemed quite to take to her; she declared he was admiring the real lace on her cap, but Mary thought (though she did not say so) that he was pleased by her kind looks and coaxing words. Then he was wrapped up and carried carefully upstairs to tea, in Mrs Jenkins's room. And after tea, Mrs Jenkins, and Mary, and her husband, found out each other's mutual liking for music, and sat singing old glees and catches, till I don't know what o'clock, without one word of politics or newspapers.

Before they parted, Mary had coaxed pussy on to her knee; for Mrs Jenkins would not part with baby, who was sleeping on her lap.

"When you're busy, bring him to me. Do, now, it will be a real favour. I know you must have a deal to do, with another coming; let him come up to me. I'll take the greatest of cares of him; pretty darling, how sweet he looks when he's asleep!"

When the couples were once more alone, the husbands unburdened their minds to their wives.

Mr Jenkins said to his – "Do you know, Burgess tried to make me believe Hodgson was such a fool as to put paragraphs into the *Examiner* now and then; but I see he knows his place, and has got too much sense to do any such thing."

Hodgson said – "Mary, love, I almost fancy from Jenkins's way of speaking (so much civiler than I expected), he guesses I wrote that 'Pro Bono' and the 'Rose-bud,' – at any rate, I've no objection to your naming it, if the subject should come uppermost; I should like him to know I'm a literary man."

Well! I've ended my tale; I hope you don't think it too long; but, before I go, just let me say one thing.

If any of you have any quarrels, or misunderstandings, or coolnesses, or cold shoulders, or shynesses, or tiffs, or miffs, or huffs, with anyone else, just make friends before Christmas – you will be so much merrier if you do.

I ask it of you for the sake of that old angelic song, heard so many years ago by the shepherds, keeping watch by night, on Bethlehem Heights.

"The Snow Queen"
by Hans Christian Andersen

"The Snow Queen" is not only the longest story in this collection, it is also the only one that is not specifically about Christmas. And yet it's easy to see why Hans Christian Andersen's classic fairy tale has become part of festive tradition, with its exciting tale of the little girl Gerda who travels to Lapland on the back of a reindeer to rescue her friend from the villainous Snow Queen.

The story has been popular ever since it was first published in 1845, and has inspired numerous movie and television adaptations. It's the perfect tale for cold, snowy December nights.

FIRST STORY

Which Treats of a Mirror and of the Splinters

Now then, let us begin. When we are at the end of the story, we shall know more than we know now: but to begin.

Once upon a time there was a wicked sprite, indeed he was the most mischievous of all sprites. One day he was in a very good humour, for he had made a mirror with the power of causing all that was good and beautiful when it was reflected therein, to look poor and mean; but that which was good-for-nothing and looked ugly was shown magnified and increased in ugliness. In this mirror the most beautiful landscapes looked like boiled spinach, and the best persons were turned into frights, or appeared to stand on their heads;

their faces were so distorted that they were not to be recognized; and if anyone had a mole, you might be sure that it would be magnified and spread over both nose and mouth.

"That's glorious fun!" said the sprite. If a good thought passed through a man's mind, then a grin was seen in the mirror, and the sprite laughed heartily at his clever discovery. All the little sprites who went to his school – for he kept a sprite school – told each other that a miracle had happened; and that now only, as they thought, it would be possible to see how the world really looked. They ran about with the mirror; and at last there was not a land or a person who was not represented distorted in the mirror. So then they thought they would fly up to the sky, and have a joke there. The higher they flew with the mirror, the more terribly it grinned: they could hardly hold it fast. Higher and higher still they flew, nearer and nearer to the stars, when suddenly the mirror shook so terribly with grinning, that it flew out of their hands and fell to the earth, where it was dashed in a hundred million and more pieces. And now it worked much more evil than before; for some of these pieces were hardly so large as a grain of sand, and they flew about in the wide world, and when they got into people's eyes, there they stayed; and then people saw everything perverted, or only had an eye for that which was evil. This happened because the very smallest bit had the same power which the whole mirror had possessed. Some persons even got a splinter in their heart, and then it made one shudder, for their heart became like a lump of ice. Some of the broken pieces were so large that they were used for windowpanes, through which one could not see one's friends. Other pieces were put in spectacles; and that was a sad affair when people put on their glasses to see well and rightly. Then the wicked sprite laughed till he almost choked, for all this tickled his fancy. The fine splinters still flew about in the air: and now we shall hear what happened next.

SECOND STORY

A Little Boy and a Little Girl

In a large town, where there are so many houses, and so many people, that there is no room left for everybody to have a little garden; and where, on this account, most persons are obliged to content themselves with flowers in pots; there lived two little children, who had a garden somewhat larger than a flowerpot. They were not brother and sister; but they cared for each other as much as if they were. Their parents lived exactly opposite. They inhabited two garrets; and where the roof of the one house joined that of the other, and the gutter ran along the extreme end of it, there was to each house a small window: one needed only to step over the gutter to get from one window to the other.

The children's parents had large wooden boxes there, in which vegetables for the kitchen were planted, and little rose trees besides: there was a rose in each box, and they grew splendidly. They now thought of placing the boxes across the gutter, so that they nearly reached from one window to the other, and looked just like two walls of flowers. The tendrils of the peas hung down over the boxes; and the rosetrees shot up long branches, twined round the windows, and then bent towards each other: it was almost like a triumphant arch of foliage and flowers. The boxes were very high, and the children knew that they must not creep over them; so they often obtained permission to get out of the windows to each other, and to sit on their little stools among the roses, where they could play delightfully. In winter there was an end of this pleasure. The windows were often frozen over; but then they heated copper farthings on the stove, and laid the hot farthing on the windowpane, and then they had a capital peephole, quite nicely rounded; and out of each peeped a gentle friendly eye – it was the little boy and the little girl who were looking out. His name was Kay, hers was Gerda. In summer, with one jump, they could get to each other; but in winter they were obliged first to go down the long stairs, and then up the long stairs again: and out-of-doors there was quite a snow-storm.

"It is the white bees that are swarming," said Kay's old grandmother.

"Do the white bees choose a queen?" asked the little boy; for he knew that the honey-bees always have one.

"Yes," said the grandmother, "she flies where the swarm hangs in the thickest clusters. She is the largest of all; and she can never remain quietly on the earth, but goes up again into the black clouds. Many a winter's night she flies through the streets of the town, and peeps in at the windows; and they then freeze in so wondrous a manner that they look like flowers."

"Yes, I have seen it," said both the children; and so they knew that it was true.

"Can the Snow Queen come in?" said the little girl.

"Only let her come in!" said the little boy. "Then I'd put her on the stove, and she'd melt."

And then his grandmother patted his head and told him other stories.

In the evening, when little Kay was at home, and half undressed, he climbed up on the chair by the window, and peeped out of the little hole. A few snowflakes were falling, and one, the largest of all, remained lying on the edge of a flowerpot.

The flake of snow grew larger and larger; and at last it was like a young lady, dressed in the finest white gauze, made of a million little flakes like stars. She was so beautiful and delicate, but she was of ice, of dazzling, sparkling ice; yet she lived; her eyes gazed fixedly, like two stars; but there was neither quiet nor repose in them. She nodded towards the window, and beckoned with her hand. The little boy was frightened, and jumped down from the chair; it seemed to him as if, at the same moment, a large bird flew past the window.

The next day it was a sharp frost – and then the spring came; the sun shone, the green leaves appeared, the swallows built their nests, the windows were opened, and the little children again sat in their pretty garden, high up on the leads at the top of the house.

That summer the roses flowered in unwonted beauty. The little girl had learned a hymn, in which there was something about roses; and then she thought of her own flowers; and she sang the verse to the little boy, who then sang it with her:

"The rose in the valley is blooming so sweet,
And angels descend there the children to
greet."

And the children held each other by the hand, kissed the roses, looked up at the clear sunshine, and spoke as though they really saw angels there. What lovely summer-days those were! How delightful to be out in the air, near the fresh rose-bushes, that seem as if they would never finish blossoming!

Kay and Gerda looked at the picture book full of beasts and of birds; and it was then – the clock in the church-tower was just striking five – that Kay said, "Oh! I feel such a sharp pain in my heart; and now something has got into my eye!"

The little girl put her arms around his neck. He winked his eyes; now there was nothing to be seen.

"I think it is out now," said he; but it was not. It was just one of those pieces of glass from the magic mirror that had got into his eye; and poor Kay had got another piece right in his heart. It will soon become like ice. It did not hurt any longer, but there it was.

"What are you crying for?" asked he. "You look so ugly! There's nothing the matter with me. Ah," said he at once, "that rose is cankered! And look, this one is quite crooked! After all, these roses are very ugly! They are just like the box they are planted in!" And then he gave the box a good kick with his foot, and pulled both the roses up.

"What are you doing?" cried the little girl; and as he perceived her fright, he pulled up another rose, got in at the window, and hastened off from dear little Gerda.

Afterwards, when she brought her picture book, he asked, "What horrid beasts have you there?" And if his grandmother told them stories, he always interrupted her; besides, if he could manage it, he would get behind her, put on her spectacles, and imitate her way of speaking; he copied all her ways, and then everybody laughed at him. He was soon able to imitate the gait and manner of everyone in the street. Everything that was peculiar and displeasing in them – that Kay knew how to imitate: and at such times all the people said, "The boy is certainly very clever!" But it was the glass he had got in his eye; the glass that was sticking in his heart, which made him tease even little Gerda, whose whole soul was devoted to him.

His games now were quite different to what they had formerly been, they were so very knowing. One winter's day, when the flakes of snow were flying about, he spread the skirts of his blue coat, and caught the snow as it fell.

"Look through this glass, Gerda," said he. And every flake seemed larger, and appeared like a magnificent flower, or beautiful star; it was splendid to look at!

"Look, how clever!" said Kay. "That's much more interesting than real flowers! They are as exact as possible; there is not a fault in them, if they did not melt!"

It was not long after this, that Kay came one day with large gloves on, and his little sledge at his back, and bawled right into Gerda's ears, "I have permission to go out into the square where the others are playing"; and off he was in a moment.

There, in the market-place, some of the boldest of the boys used to tie their sledges to the carts as they passed by, and so they were pulled along, and got a good ride. It was so capital! Just as they were in the very height of their amusement, a large sledge passed by: it was painted quite white, and there was someone in it wrapped up in a rough white mantle of fur, with a rough white fur cap on his head. The sledge drove round the square twice, and Kay tied on his sledge as quickly as he could, and off he drove with it. On they went quicker and quicker into the next street; and the person who drove turned round to Kay, and nodded to him in a friendly manner, just as if they knew each other. Every time he was going to untie his sledge, the person nodded to him, and then Kay sat quiet; and so on they went till they came outside the gates of the town. Then the snow began to fall so thickly that the little boy could not see an arm's length before him, but still on he went: when suddenly he let go the string he held in his hand in order to get loose from the sledge, but it was of no use; still the little vehicle rushed on with the quickness of the wind. He then cried as loud as he could, but no one heard him; the snow drifted and the sledge flew on, and sometimes it gave a jerk as though they were driving over hedges and ditches. He was quite frightened, and he tried to repeat the Lord's Prayer; but all he could do, he was only able to remember the multiplication table.

The snowflakes grew larger and larger, till at last they looked just like great white fowls. Suddenly they flew on one side; the large sledge stopped, and the person who drove rose up. It was a lady; her cloak and cap were of snow. She was tall and of slender figure, and of a dazzling whiteness. It was the Snow Queen.

"We have travelled fast," said she; "but it is freezingly cold. Come under my bearskin." And she put him in the sledge beside her, wrapped the fur round him, and he felt as though he were sinking in a snow-wreath.

"Are you still cold?" asked she; and then she kissed his forehead. Ah! it was colder than ice; it penetrated to his very heart, which was already almost a frozen lump; it seemed to him as if he were about to die – but a moment more and it was quite congenial to him, and he did not remark the cold that was around him.

"My sledge! Do not forget my sledge!" It was the first thing he thought of. It was there tied to one of the white chickens, who flew along with it on his back behind the large sledge. The Snow Queen kissed Kay once more, and then he forgot little Gerda, grandmother, and all whom he had left at his home.

"Now you will have no more kisses," said she, "or else I should kiss you to death!"

Kay looked at her. She was very beautiful; a more clever, or a more lovely countenance he could not fancy to himself; and she no longer appeared of ice as before, when she sat outside the window, and beckoned to him; in his eyes she was perfect, he did not fear her at all, and told her that he could calculate in his head and with fractions, even; that he knew the number of square miles there were in the different countries, and how many inhabitants they contained; and she smiled while he spoke. It then seemed to him as if what he knew was not enough, and he looked upwards in the large huge empty space above him, and on she flew with him; flew high over the black clouds, while the storm moaned and whistled as though it were singing some old tune. On they flew over woods and lakes, over seas, and many lands; and beneath them the chilling storm rushed fast, the wolves howled, the snow crackled; above them flew large screaming crows, but higher up appeared the moon, quite large and bright; and it was on it that Kay gazed during the long long winter's night; while by day he slept at the feet of the Snow Queen.

THIRD STORY

Of the Flower-Garden At the Old Woman's
Who Understood Witchcraft

But what became of little Gerda when Kay did not
return? Where could he be? Nobody knew; nobody
could give any intelligence. All the boys knew was, that
they had seen him tie his sledge to another large and
splendid one, which drove down the street and out of
the town. Nobody knew where he was; many sad tears
were shed, and little Gerda wept long and bitterly; at last
she said he must be dead; that he had been drowned
in the river which flowed close to the town. Oh! those
were very long and dismal winter evenings!

At last spring came, with its warm sunshine.

"Kay is dead and gone!" said little Gerda.

"That I don't believe," said the Sunshine.

"Kay is dead and gone!" said she to the Swallows.

"That I don't believe," said they: and at last little
Gerda did not think so any longer either.

"I'll put on my red shoes," said she, one morning;
"Kay has never seen them, and then I'll go down to the
river and ask there."

It was quite early; she kissed her old grandmother,

who was still asleep, put on her red shoes, and went alone to the river.

"Is it true that you have taken my little playfellow? I will make you a present of my red shoes, if you will give him back to me."

And, as it seemed to her, the blue waves nodded in a strange manner; then she took off her red shoes, the most precious things she possessed, and threw them both into the river. But they fell close to the bank, and the little waves bore them immediately to land; it was as if the stream would not take what was dearest to her; for in reality it had not got little Kay; but Gerda thought that she had not thrown the shoes out far enough, so she clambered into a boat which lay among the rushes, went to the farthest end, and threw out the shoes. But the boat was not fastened, and the motion which she occasioned, made it drift from the shore. She observed this, and hastened to get back; but before she could do so, the boat was more than a yard from the land, and was gliding quickly onward.

Little Gerda was very frightened, and began to cry; but no one heard her except the sparrows, and they could not carry her to land; but they flew along the bank, and sang as if to comfort her, "Here we are! Here we are!" The boat drifted with the stream, little Gerda sat quite still without shoes, for they were swimming behind the boat, but she could not reach them, because the boat went much faster than they did.

The banks on both sides were beautiful; lovely flowers, venerable trees, and slopes with sheep and cows, but not a human being was to be seen.

"Perhaps the river will carry me to little Kay," said she; and then she grew less sad. She rose, and looked for many hours at the beautiful green banks. Presently she sailed by a large cherry-orchard, where was a little cottage with curious red and blue windows; it was thatched, and before it two wooden soldiers stood sentry, and presented arms when anyone went past.

Gerda called to them, for she thought they were alive; but they, of course, did not answer. She came close to them, for the stream drifted the boat quite near the land.

Gerda called still louder, and an old woman then came out of the cottage, leaning upon a crooked stick. She had a large broad-brimmed hat on, painted with the most splendid flowers.

"Poor little child!" said the old woman. "How did you get upon the large rapid river, to be driven about so in the wide world!" And then the old woman went into the water, caught hold of the boat with her crooked stick, drew it to the bank, and lifted little Gerda out.

And Gerda was so glad to be on dry land again; but she was rather afraid of the strange old woman.

"But come and tell me who you are, and how you came here," said she.

And Gerda told her all; and the old woman shook her head and said, "A-hem! a-hem!" and when Gerda had told her everything, and asked her if she had not seen little Kay, the woman answered that he had not passed there, but he no doubt would come; and she told her not to be cast down, but taste her cherries, and look at her flowers, which were finer than any in a picture book, each of which could tell a whole story. She then took Gerda by the hand, led her into the little cottage, and locked the door.

The windows were very high up; the glass was red, blue, and green, and the sunlight shone through quite wondrously in all sorts of colours. On the table stood the most exquisite cherries, and Gerda ate as many as she chose, for she had permission to do so. While she was eating, the old woman combed her hair with a golden comb, and her hair curled and shone with a lovely golden colour around that sweet little face, which was so round and so like a rose.

"I have often longed for such a dear little girl," said the old woman. "Now you shall see how well we agree together"; and while she combed little Gerda's hair, the child forgot her foster-brother Kay more and more, for the old woman understood magic; but she was no evil being, she only practised witchcraft a little for her own private amusement, and now she wanted very much to keep little Gerda. She therefore went out in the garden, stretched out her crooked stick towards the rose bushes, which, beautifully as they were blowing, all sank into the earth and no one could tell where they had stood. The old woman feared that if Gerda should see the roses, she would then think of her own, would remember little Kay, and run away from her.

She now led Gerda into the flower garden. Oh, what odour and what loveliness was there! Every flower that one could think of, and of every season, stood there in fullest bloom; no picture book could be gayer or more beautiful. Gerda jumped for joy, and played till the sun set behind the tall cherry tree; she then had a pretty bed, with a red silken coverlet filled with blue violets.

She fell asleep, and had as pleasant dreams as ever a queen on her wedding-day.

The next morning she went to play with the flowers in the warm sunshine, and thus passed away a day. Gerda knew every flower; and, numerous as they were, it still seemed to Gerda that one was wanting, though she did not know which. One day while she was looking at the hat of the old woman painted with flowers, the most beautiful of them all seemed to her to be a rose. The old woman had forgotten to take it from her hat when she made the others vanish in the earth. But so it is when one's thoughts are not collected. "What!" said Gerda. "Are there no roses here?" and she ran about amongst the flowerbeds, and looked, and looked, but there was not one to be found. She then sat down and wept; but her hot tears fell just where a rose bush had sunk; and when her warm tears watered the ground, the tree shot up suddenly as fresh and blooming as when it had been swallowed up. Gerda kissed the roses, thought of her own dear roses at home, and with them of little Kay.

"Oh, how long I have stayed!" said the little girl. "I intended to look for Kay! Don't you know where he is?" she asked of the roses. "Do you think he is dead and gone?"

"Dead he certainly is not," said the Roses. "We have been in the earth where all the dead are, but Kay was not there."

"Many thanks!" said little Gerda; and she went to the other flowers, looked into their cups, and asked, "Don't you know where little Kay is?"

But every flower stood in the sunshine, and dreamed its own fairy tale or its own story: and they all told her very many things, but not one knew anything of Kay.

Well, what did the Tiger-Lily say?

"Hearest thou not the drum? Bum! Bum! Those are the only two tones. Always bum! Bum! Hark to the plaintive song of the old woman, to the call of the priests! The Hindoo woman in her long robe stands upon the funeral pile; the flames rise around her and her dead husband, but the Hindoo woman thinks on the living one in the surrounding circle; on him whose eyes burn hotter than the flames – on him, the fire of whose eyes pierces her heart more than the flames which soon will burn her body to ashes. Can the heart's flame die in the flame of the funeral pile?"

"I don't understand that at all," said little Gerda.

"That is my story," said the Lily.

What did the Convolvulus say?

"Projecting over a narrow mountain-path there hangs an old feudal castle. Thick evergreens grow on the dilapidated walls, and around the altar, where a lovely maiden is standing: she bends over the railing and looks out upon the rose. No fresher rose hangs on the branches than she; no appleblossom carried away by the wind is more buoyant! How her silken robe is rustling!

"'Is he not yet come?'"

"Is it Kay that you mean?" asked little Gerda.

"I am speaking about my story – about my dream," answered the Convolvulus.

What did the Snowdrops say?

"Between the trees a long board is hanging – it is a swing. Two little girls are sitting in it, and swing themselves backwards and forwards; their frocks are as white as snow, and long green silk ribands flutter from their bonnets. Their brother, who is older than they are, stands up in the swing; he twines his arms round the cords to hold himself fast, for in one hand he has a little cup, and in the other a clay-pipe. He is blowing soap bubbles. The swing moves, and the bubbles float in charming changing colours: the last is still hanging to the end of the pipe, and rocks in the breeze. The swing moves. The little black dog, as light as a soap bubble, jumps up on his hind legs to try to get into the swing. It moves, the dog falls down, barks, and is angry. They tease him; the bubble bursts! A swing, a bursting bubble – such is my song!"

"What you relate may be very pretty, but you tell it in so melancholy a manner, and do not mention Kay."

What do the Hyacinths say?

"There were once upon a time three sisters, quite transparent, and very beautiful. The robe of the one was red, that of the second blue, and that of the third white. They danced hand in hand beside the calm lake in the clear moonshine. They were not elfin maidens, but mortal children. A sweet fragrance was smelt, and the maidens vanished in the wood; the fragrance grew stronger – three coffins, and in them three lovely maidens, glided out of the forest and across the lake: the shining glowworms flew around like little floating lights. Do the dancing maidens sleep, or are they dead? The odour of the flowers says they are corpses; the evening bell tolls for the dead!"

"You make me quite sad," said little Gerda. "I cannot help thinking of the dead maidens. Oh! is little Kay really dead? The Roses have been in the earth, and they say no."

"Ding, dong!" sounded the Hyacinth bells. "We do not toll for little Kay; we do not know him. That is our way of singing, the only one we have."

And Gerda went to the Ranunculuses, that looked forth from among the shining green leaves.

"You are a little bright sun!" said Gerda. "Tell me if you know where I can find my playfellow."

And the Ranunculus shone brightly, and looked again at Gerda. What song could the Ranunculus sing? It was one that said nothing about Kay either.

"In a small court the bright sun was shining in the first days of spring. The beams glided down the white walls of a neighbor's house, and close by the fresh yellow flowers were growing, shining like gold in the warm sun-rays. An old grandmother was sitting in the air; her grand-daughter, the poor and lovely servant just come for a short visit. She knows her grandmother. There was gold, pure virgin gold in that blessed kiss. There, that is my little story," said the Ranunculus.

"My poor old grandmother!" sighed Gerda. "Yes, she is longing for me, no doubt: she is sorrowing for me, as she did for little Kay. But I will soon come home, and then I will bring Kay with me. It is of no use asking the flowers; they only know their own old rhymes, and can tell me nothing." And she tucked up her frock, to enable her to run quicker; but the Narcissus gave her a knock on the leg, just as she was going to jump over it. So she stood still, looked at the long yellow flower, and asked, "You perhaps know something?" and she bent down to the Narcissus. And what did it say?

"I can see myself – I can see myself! Oh, how odorous I am! Up in the little garret there stands, half-dressed, a little Dancer. She stands now on one leg, now on both; she despises the whole world; yet she lives only in imagination. She pours water out of the teapot over a piece of stuff which she holds in her hand; it is the bodice; cleanliness is a fine thing. The white dress is hanging on the hook; it was washed in the teapot, and dried on the roof. She puts it on, ties a saffron-coloured kerchief round her neck, and then the gown looks whiter. I can see myself – I can see myself!"

"That's nothing to me," said little Gerda. "That does not concern me." And then off she ran to the further end of the garden.

The gate was locked, but she shook the rusted bolt till it was loosened, and the gate opened; and little Gerda ran off barefooted into the wide world. She looked round her thrice, but no one followed her. At last she could run no longer; she sat down on a large stone, and when she looked about her, she saw that the summer had passed; it was late in the autumn, but that one could not remark in the beautiful garden, where there was always sunshine, and where there were flowers the whole year round.

"Dear me, how long I have staid!" said Gerda. "Autumn is come. I must not rest any longer." And she got up to go further.

Oh, how tender and wearied her little feet were! All around it looked so cold and raw: the long willow-leaves were quite yellow, and the fog dripped from them like water; one leaf fell after the other: the sloes only stood full of fruit, which set one's teeth on edge. Oh, how dark and comfortless it was in the dreary world!

FOURTH STORY

The Prince and Princess

Gerda was obliged to rest herself again, when, exactly opposite to her, a large Raven came hopping over the white snow. He had long been looking at Gerda and shaking his head; and now he said, "Caw! Caw!" Good day! Good day! He could not say it better; but he felt a sympathy for the little girl, and asked her where she was going all alone. The word "alone" Gerda understood quite well, and felt how much was expressed by it; so she told the Raven her whole history, and asked if he had not seen Kay.

The Raven nodded very gravely, and said, "It may be – it may be!"

"What, do you really think so?" cried the little girl; and she nearly squeezed the Raven to death, so much did she kiss him.

"Gently, gently," said the Raven. "I think I know; I think that it may be little Kay. But now he has forgotten you for the Princess."

"Does he live with a Princess?" asked Gerda.

"Yes – listen," said the Raven; "but it will be difficult for me to speak your language. If you understand the Raven language I can tell you better."

"No, I have not learnt it," said Gerda; "but my grandmother understands it, and she can speak gibberish too. I wish I had learnt it."

"No matter," said the Raven; "I will tell you as well as I can; however, it will be bad enough." And then he told all he knew.

"In the kingdom where we now are there lives a Princess, who is extraordinarily clever; for she has read all the newspapers in the whole world, and has forgotten them again – so clever is she. She was lately, it is said, sitting on her throne – which is not very amusing after all – when she began humming an old tune, and it was just, 'Oh, why should I not be married?' 'That song is not without its meaning,' said she, and so then she was determined to marry; but she would have a husband who knew how to give an answer when he was spoken to – not one who looked only as if he were a great personage, for that is so tiresome. She then had all the ladies of the court drummed together; and when they heard her intention, all were very pleased, and said, 'We are very glad to hear it; it is the very thing we were thinking of.' You may believe every word I say," said the Raven; "for I have a tame sweetheart that hops about in the palace quite free, and it was she who told me all this.

"The newspapers appeared forthwith with a border of hearts and the initials of the Princess; and therein you might read that every good-looking young man was at liberty to come to the palace and speak to the Princess; and he who spoke in such wise as showed he felt himself at home there, that one the Princess would choose for her husband.

"Yes, Yes," said the Raven, "you may believe it; it is as true as I am sitting here. People came in crowds; there was a crush and a hurry, but no one was successful either on the first or second day. They could all talk well enough when they were out in the street; but as soon as they came inside the palace gates, and saw the guard richly dressed in silver, and the lackeys in gold on the staircase, and the large illuminated saloons, then they were abashed; and when they stood before the throne on which the Princess was sitting, all they could do was to repeat the last word they had uttered, and to hear it again did not interest her very much. It was just as if the people within were under a charm, and had fallen into a trance till they came out again into the street; for then – oh, then – they could chatter enough. There was a whole row of them standing from the town-gates to the palace. I was there myself to look," said the Raven. "They grew hungry and thirsty; but from the palace they got nothing whatever, not even a glass of water. Some of the cleverest, it is true, had taken bread and butter with them: but none shared it with his neighbour, for each thought, 'Let him look hungry, and then the Princess won't have him.'"

"But Kay – little Kay," said Gerda, "when did he come? Was he among the number?"

"Patience, patience; we are just come to him. It was on the third day when a little personage without horse or equipage, came marching right boldly up to the palace; his eyes shone like yours, he had beautiful long hair, but his clothes were very shabby."

"That was Kay," cried Gerda, with a voice of delight. "Oh, now I've found him!" and she clapped her hands for joy.

"He had a little knapsack at his back," said the Raven.

"No, that was certainly his sledge," said Gerda; "for when he went away he took his sledge with him."

"That may be," said the Raven; "I did not examine him so minutely; but I know from my tame sweetheart, that when he came into the courtyard of the palace, and saw the body-guard in silver, the lackeys on the staircase, he was not the least abashed; he nodded, and said to them, 'It must be very tiresome to stand on the stairs; for my part, I shall go in.' The saloons were gleaming with lustres – privy councillors and excellencies were walking about barefooted, and wore gold keys; it was enough to make anyone feel uncomfortable. His boots creaked, too, so loudly, but still he was not at all afraid."

"That's Kay for certain," said Gerda. "I know he had on new boots; I have heard them creaking in grandmama's room."

"Yes, they creaked," said the Raven. "And on he went boldly up to the Princess, who was sitting on a pearl as large as a spinning-wheel. All the ladies of the court, with their attendants and attendants' attendants, and all the cavaliers, with their gentlemen and gentlemen's gentlemen, stood round; and the nearer they stood to the door, the prouder they looked. It was hardly possible to look at the gentleman's gentleman, so very haughtily did he stand in the doorway."

"It must have been terrible," said little Gerda. "And did Kay get the Princess?"

"Were I not a Raven, I should have taken the Princess myself, although I am promised. It is said he spoke as well as I speak when I talk Raven language; this I learned from my tame sweetheart. He was bold and nicely behaved; he had not come to woo the Princess, but only to hear her wisdom. She pleased him, and he pleased her."

"Yes, yes; for certain that was Kay," said Gerda. "He was so clever; he could reckon fractions in his head. Oh, won't you take me to the palace?"

"That is very easily said," answered the Raven. "But how are we to manage it? I'll speak to my tame sweetheart about it: she must advise us; for so much I must tell you, such a little girl as you are will never get permission to enter."

"Oh, yes I shall," said Gerda; "when Kay hears that I am here, he will come out directly to fetch me."

"Wait for me here on these steps," said the Raven. He moved his head backwards and forwards and flew away.

The evening was closing in when the Raven returned. "Caw – caw!" said he. "She sends you her compliments; and here is a roll for you. She took it out of the kitchen, where there is bread enough. You are hungry, no doubt. It is not possible for you to enter the palace, for you are barefooted: the guards in silver, and the lackeys in gold, would not allow it; but do not cry, you shall come in still. My sweetheart knows a little back stair that leads to the bedchamber, and she knows where she can get the key of it."

And they went into the garden in the large avenue, where one leaf was falling after the other; and when the lights in the palace had all gradually disappeared, the Raven led little Gerda to the back door, which stood half open.

Oh, how Gerda's heart beat with anxiety and longing! It was just as if she had been about to do something wrong; and yet she only wanted to know if little Kay was there. Yes, he must be there. She called to mind his intelligent eyes, and his long hair, so vividly, she could quite see him as he used to laugh when they were sitting under the roses at home. "He will, no doubt, be glad to see you – to hear what a long way you have come for his sake; to know how unhappy all at home were when he did not come back."

Oh, what a fright and a joy it was!

They were now on the stairs. A single lamp was burning there; and on the floor stood the tame Raven, turning her head on every side and looking at Gerda, who bowed as her grandmother had taught her to do.

"My intended has told me so much good of you, my dear young lady," said the tame Raven. "Your tale is very affecting. If you will take the lamp, I will go before. We will go straight on, for we shall meet no one."

"I think there is somebody just behind us," said Gerda; and something rushed past: it was like shadowy figures on the wall; horses with flowing manes and thin legs, huntsmen, ladies and gentlemen on horseback.

"They are only dreams," said the Raven. "They come

to fetch the thoughts of the high personages to the chase; 'tis well, for now you can observe them in bed all the better. But let me find, when you enjoy honour and distinction, that you possess a grateful heart."

"Tut! That's not worth talking about," said the Raven of the woods.

They now entered the first saloon, which was of rose-coloured satin, with artificial flowers on the wall. Here the dreams were rushing past, but they hastened by so quickly that Gerda could not see the high personages. One hall was more magnificent than the other; one might indeed well be abashed; and at last they came into the bedchamber. The ceiling of the room resembled a large palm-tree with leaves of glass, of costly glass; and in the middle, from a thick golden stem, hung two beds, each of which resembled a lily. One was white, and in this lay the Princess; the other was red, and it was here that Gerda was to look for little Kay. She bent back one of the red leaves, and saw a brown neck. Oh! that was Kay! She called him quite loud by name, held the lamp towards him – the dreams rushed back again into the chamber – he awoke, turned his head, and – it was not little Kay!

The Prince was only like him about the neck; but

he was young and handsome. And out of the white lily leaves the Princess peeped, too, and asked what was the matter. Then little Gerda cried, and told her her whole history, and all that the Ravens had done for her.

"Poor little thing!" said the Prince and the Princess. They praised the Ravens very much, and told them they were not at all angry with them, but they were not to do so again. However, they should have a reward. "Will you fly about here at liberty," asked the Princess; "or would you like to have a fixed appointment as court ravens, with all the broken bits from the kitchen?"

And both the Ravens nodded, and begged for a fixed appointment; for they thought of their old age, and said, "It is a good thing to have a provision for our old days."

And the Prince got up and let Gerda sleep in his bed, and more than this he could not do. She folded her little hands and thought, "How good men and animals are!" and she then fell asleep and slept soundly. All the dreams flew in again, and they now looked like the angels; they drew a little sledge, in which little Kay sat and nodded his head; but the whole was only a dream, and therefore it all vanished as soon as she awoke.

The next day she was dressed from head to foot in silk and velvet. They offered to let her stay at the palace, and lead a happy life; but she begged to have a little carriage with a horse in front, and for a small pair of shoes; then, she said, she would again go forth in the wide world and look for Kay.

Shoes and a muff were given her; she was, too, dressed very nicely; and when she was about to set off, a new carriage stopped before the door. It was of pure gold, and the arms of the Prince and Princess shone like a star upon it; the coachman, the footmen, and the outriders, for outriders were there, too, all wore golden crowns. The Prince and the Princess assisted her into the carriage themselves, and wished her all success. The Raven of the woods, who was now married, accompanied her for the first three miles. He sat beside Gerda, for he could not bear riding backwards; the other Raven stood in the doorway, and flapped her wings; she could not accompany Gerda, because she suffered from headache since she had had a fixed appointment and ate so much. The carriage was lined inside with sugar-plums, and in the seats were fruits and gingerbread.

"Farewell! Farewell!" cried Prince and Princess; and Gerda wept, and the Raven wept. Thus passed the first miles; and then the Raven bade her farewell, and this was the most painful separation of all. He flew into a tree, and beat his black wings as long as he could see the carriage, that shone from afar like a sunbeam.

FIFTH STORY

The Little Robber Maiden

They drove through the dark wood; but the carriage shone like a torch, and it dazzled the eyes of the robbers, so that they could not bear to look at it.

"'Tis gold! 'Tis gold!" they cried; and they rushed forward, seized the horses, knocked down the little postilion, the coachman, and the servants, and pulled little Gerda out of the carriage.

"How plump, how beautiful she is! She must have been fed on nut-kernels," said the old female robber, who had a long, scrubby beard, and bushy eyebrows that hung down over her eyes. "She is as good as a fatted lamb! How nice she will be!" And then she drew out a knife, the blade of which shone so that it was quite dreadful to behold.

"Oh!" cried the woman at the same moment. She had been bitten in the ear by her own little daughter, who hung at her back; and who was so wild and unmanageable, that it was quite amusing to see her. "You naughty child!" said the mother: and now she had not time to kill Gerda.

"She shall play with me," said the little robber child. "She shall give me her muff, and her pretty frock; she shall sleep in my bed!" And then she gave her mother another bite, so that she jumped, and ran round with the pain; and the Robbers laughed, and said, "Look, how she is dancing with the little one!"

"I will go into the carriage," said the little robber maiden; and she would have her will, for she was very spoiled and very headstrong. She and Gerda got in; and then away they drove over the stumps of felled trees, deeper and deeper into the woods. The little robber maiden was as tall as Gerda, but stronger, broader-shouldered, and of dark complexion; her eyes were quite black; they looked almost melancholy. She embraced little Gerda, and said, "They shall not kill you as long as I am not displeased with you. You are, doubtless, a Princess?"

"No," said little Gerda; who then related all that had happened to her, and how much she cared about little Kay.

The little robber maiden looked at her with a serious air, nodded her head slightly, and said, "They shall not kill you, even if I am angry with you: then I will do it myself"; and she dried Gerda's eyes, and put both her hands in the handsome muff, which was so soft and warm.

At length the carriage stopped. They were in the midst of the courtyard of a robber's castle. It was full of cracks from top to bottom; and out of the openings magpies and rooks were flying; and the great bull-dogs, each of which looked as if he could swallow a man, jumped up, but they did not bark, for that was forbidden.

In the midst of the large, old, smoking hall burnt a great fire on the stone floor. The smoke disappeared under the stones, and had to seek its own egress. In an immense caldron soup was boiling; and rabbits and hares were being roasted on a spit.

"You shall sleep with me tonight, with all my animals," said the little robber maiden. They had something to eat and drink; and then went into a corner, where straw and carpets were lying. Beside them, on laths and perches, sat nearly a hundred pigeons, all asleep, seemingly; but yet they moved a little when the robber maiden came. "They are all mine," said she, at the same time seizing one that was next to her by the legs and shaking it so that its wings fluttered. "Kiss it," cried the little girl, and flung the pigeon in Gerda's face. "Up there is the rabble of the wood," continued she, pointing to several laths which were fastened before a hole high up in the wall; "that's the rabble; they would all fly away immediately, if they were not well fastened in. And here is my dear old Bac"; and she laid hold of the horns of a reindeer, that had a bright copper ring round its neck, and was tethered to the spot. "We are obliged to lock this fellow in too, or he would make his escape. Every evening I tickle his neck with my sharp knife; he is so frightened at it!" and the little girl drew forth a long knife, from a crack in the wall, and let it glide over the Reindeer's neck. The poor animal kicked; the girl laughed, and pulled Gerda into bed with her.

"Do you intend to keep your knife while you sleep?" asked Gerda; looking at it rather fearfully.

"I always sleep with the knife," said the little robber maiden. "There is no knowing what may happen. But tell me now, once more, all about little Kay; and why you have started off in the wide world alone." And Gerda related all, from the very beginning: the Wood-pigeons cooed above in their cage, and the others slept. The little robber maiden wound her arm round Gerda's neck, held the knife in the other hand, and snored so loud that everybody could hear her; but Gerda could not close her eyes, for she did not know whether she was to live or die. The robbers sat round the fire, sang and drank; and the old female robber jumped about so, that it was quite dreadful for Gerda to see her.

Then the Wood-pigeons said, "Coo! Coo! We have seen little Kay! A white hen carries his sledge; he himself sat in the carriage of the Snow Queen, who passed here, down just over the wood, as we lay in our nest. She blew upon us young ones; and all died except we two. Coo! Coo!"

"What is that you say up there?" cried little Gerda. "Where did the Snow Queen go to? Do you know anything about it?"

"She is no doubt gone to Lapland; for there is always snow and ice there. Only ask the Reindeer, who is tethered there."

"Ice and snow is there! There it is, glorious and beautiful!" said the Reindeer. "One can spring about in the large shining valleys! The Snow Queen has her summer-tent there; but her fixed abode is high up towards the North Pole, on the Island called Spitzbergen."

"Oh, Kay! Poor little Kay!" sighed Gerda.

"Do you choose to be quiet?" said the robber maiden. "If you don't, I shall make you."

In the morning Gerda told her all that the Wood-pigeons had said; and the little maiden looked very serious, but she nodded her head, and said, "That's no matter – that's no matter. Do you know where Lapland lies!" she asked of the Reindeer.

"Who should know better than I?" said the animal; and his eyes rolled in his head. "I was born and bred there – there I leapt about on the fields of snow."

"Listen," said the robber maiden to Gerda. "You see that the men are gone; but my mother is still here, and will remain. However, towards morning she takes a draught out of the large flask, and then she sleeps a little: then I will do something for you." She now jumped out of bed, flew to her mother; with her arms round her neck, and pulling her by the beard, said, "Good morrow, my own sweet nanny-goat of a mother." And her mother took hold of her nose, and pinched it till it was red and blue; but this was all done out of pure love.

When the mother had taken a sup at her flask, and was having a nap, the little robber maiden went to the Reindeer, and said, "I should very much like to give you still many a tickling with the sharp knife, for then you are so amusing; however, I will untether you, and help you out, so that you may go back to Lapland. But you must make good use of your legs; and take this little girl for me to the palace of the Snow Queen, where her playfellow is. You have heard, I suppose, all she said; for she spoke loud enough, and you were listening."

The Reindeer gave a bound for joy. The robber maiden lifted up little Gerda, and took the precaution to bind her fast on the Reindeer's back; she even gave her a small cushion to sit on. "Here are your worsted leggins, for it will be cold; but the muff I shall keep for myself, for it is so very pretty. But I do not wish you to be cold. Here is a pair of lined gloves of my mother's; they just reach up to your elbow. On with them! Now you look about the hands just like my ugly old mother!"

And Gerda wept for joy.

"I can't bear to see you fretting," said the little robber maiden. "This is just the time when you ought to look pleased. Here are two loaves and a ham for you, so that you won't starve." The bread and the meat were fastened to the Reindeer's back; the little maiden opened the door, called in all the dogs, and then with her knife cut the rope that fastened the animal, and said to him, "Now, off with you; but take good care of the little girl!"

And Gerda stretched out her hands with the large wadded gloves towards the robber maiden, and said, "Farewell!" and the Reindeer flew on over bush and bramble through the great wood, over moor and heath, as fast as he could go.

"Ddsa! Ddsa!" was heard in the sky. It was just as if somebody was sneezing.

"These are my old northern-lights," said the Reindeer, "look how they gleam!" And on he now sped still quicker – day and night on he went: the loaves were consumed, and the ham too; and now they were in Lapland.

SIXTH STORY

The Lapland Woman and the Finland Woman

Suddenly they stopped before a little house, which looked very miserable. The roof reached to the ground; and the door was so low, that the family were obliged to creep upon their stomachs when they went in or out.

Nobody was at home except an old Lapland woman, who was dressing fish by the light of an oil lamp. And the Reindeer told her the whole of Gerda's history, but first of all his own; for that seemed to him of much greater importance. Gerda was so chilled that she could not speak.

"Poor thing," said the Lapland woman, "you have far to run still. You have more than a hundred miles to go before you get to Finland; there the Snow Queen has her country-house, and burns blue lights every evening. I will give you a few words from me, which I will write on a dried haberdine, for paper I have none; this you can take with you to the Finland woman, and she will be able to give you more information than I can."

When Gerda had warmed herself, and had eaten and drunk, the Lapland woman wrote a few words on a dried haberdine, begged Gerda to take care of them, put her on the Reindeer, bound her fast, and away sprang the animal. "Ddsa! Ddsa!" was again heard in the air; the most charming blue lights burned the whole night in the sky, and at last they came to Finland. They knocked at the chimney of the Finland woman; for as to a door, she had none.

There was such a heat inside that the Finland

woman herself went about almost naked. She was diminutive and dirty. She immediately loosened little Gerda's clothes, pulled off her thick gloves and boots; for otherwise the heat would have been too great – and after laying a piece of ice on the Reindeer's head, read what was written on the fish-skin. She read it three times: she then knew it by heart; so she put the fish into the cupboard – for it might very well be eaten, and she never threw anything away.

Then the Reindeer related his own story first, and afterwards that of little Gerda; and the Finland woman winked her eyes, but said nothing.

"You are so clever," said the Reindeer; "you can, I know, twist all the winds of the world together in a knot. If the seaman loosens one knot, then he has a good wind; if a second, then it blows pretty stiffly; if he undoes the third and fourth, then it rages so that the forests are upturned. Will you give the little maiden a potion, that she may possess the strength of twelve men, and vanquish the Snow Queen?"

"The strength of twelve men!" said the Finland woman. "Much good that would be!" Then she went to a cupboard, and drew out a large skin rolled up. When she had unrolled it, strange characters were to be seen written thereon; and the Finland woman read at such a rate that the perspiration trickled down her forehead.

But the Reindeer begged so hard for little Gerda, and Gerda looked so imploringly with tearful eyes at the Finland woman, that she winked, and drew the Reindeer aside into a corner, where they whispered together, while the animal got some fresh ice put on his head.

"'Tis true little Kay is at the Snow Queen's, and finds everything there quite to his taste; and he thinks it the very best place in the world; but the reason of that is, he has a splinter of glass in his eye, and in his heart. These must be got out first; otherwise he will never go back to mankind, and the Snow Queen will retain her power over him."

"But can you give little Gerda nothing to take which will endue her with power over the whole?"

"I can give her no more power than what she has already. Don't you see how great it is? Don't you see how men and animals are forced to serve her; how well she gets through the world barefooted? She must not hear of her power from us; that power lies in her heart, because she is a sweet and innocent child! If she cannot get to the Snow Queen by herself, and rid little

Kay of the glass, we cannot help her. Two miles hence the garden of the Snow Queen begins; thither you may carry the little girl. Set her down by the large bush with red berries, standing in the snow; don't stay talking, but hasten back as fast as possible." And now the Finland woman placed little Gerda on the Reindeer's back, and off he ran with all imaginable speed.

"Oh! I have not got my boots! I have not brought my gloves!" cried little Gerda. She remarked she was without them from the cutting frost; but the Reindeer dared not stand still; on he ran till he came to the great bush with the red berries, and there he set Gerda down, kissed her mouth, while large bright tears flowed from the animal's eyes, and then back he went as fast as possible. There stood poor Gerda now, without shoes or gloves, in the very middle of dreadful icy Finland.

She ran on as fast as she could. There then came a whole regiment of snowflakes, but they did not fall from above, and they were quite bright and shining from the Aurora Borealis. The flakes ran along the ground, and the nearer they came the larger they grew. Gerda well remembered how large and strange the snowflakes appeared when she once saw them through a magnifying-glass; but now they were large and terrific in another manner – they were all alive. They were the outposts of the Snow Queen. They had the most wondrous shapes; some looked like large ugly porcupines; others like snakes knotted together, with their heads sticking out; and others, again, like small fat bears, with the hair standing on end: all were of dazzling whiteness – all were living snowflakes.

Little Gerda repeated the Lord's Prayer. The cold was so intense that she could see her own breath, which came like smoke out of her mouth. It grew thicker and thicker, and took the form of little angels, that grew more and more when they touched the earth. All had helms on their heads, and lances and shields in their hands; they increased in numbers; and when Gerda had finished the Lord's Prayer, she was surrounded by a whole legion. They thrust at the horrid snowflakes with their spears, so that they flew into a thousand pieces; and little Gerda walked on bravely and in security. The angels patted her hands and feet; and then she felt the cold less, and went on quickly towards the palace of the Snow Queen.

But now we shall see how Kay fared. He never thought of Gerda, and least of all that she was standing before the palace.

SEVENTH STORY

What Took Place in the Palace of the Snow Queen, and what Happened Afterward

The walls of the palace were of driving snow, and the windows and doors of cutting winds. There were more than a hundred halls there, according as the snow was driven by the winds. The largest was many miles in extent; all were lighted up by the powerful Aurora Borealis, and all were so large, so empty, so icy cold, and so resplendent! Mirth never reigned there; there was never even a little bear-ball, with the storm for music, while the polar bears went on their hind legs and showed off their steps. Never a little tea-party of white young lady foxes; vast, cold, and empty were the halls of the Snow Queen. The northern-lights shone with such precision that one could tell exactly when they were at their highest or lowest degree of brightness. In the middle of the empty, endless hall of snow, was a frozen lake; it was cracked in a thousand pieces, but each piece was so like the other, that it seemed the work of a cunning artificer. In the middle of this lake sat the Snow Queen when she was at home; and then she said she was sitting in the Mirror of Understanding, and that this was the only one and the best thing in the world.

Little Kay was quite blue, yes nearly black with cold; but he did not observe it, for she had kissed away all feeling of cold from his body, and his heart was a lump of ice. He was dragging along some pointed flat pieces of ice, which he laid together in all possible ways, for he wanted to make something with them; just as we have little flat pieces of wood to make geometrical figures with, called the Chinese Puzzle. Kay made all sorts of figures, the most complicated, for it was an ice-puzzle for the understanding. In his eyes the figures were extraordinarily beautiful, and of the utmost importance; for the bit of glass which was in his eye caused this. He found whole figures which represented a written word; but he never could manage to represent just the word he wanted – that word was "eternity"; and the Snow Queen had said, "If you can discover that figure, you shall be your own master, and I will make you a present of the whole world and a pair of new skates." But he could not find it out.

"I am going now to warm lands," said the Snow Queen. "I must have a look down into the black caldrons." It was the volcanoes Vesuvius and Etna that she meant. "I will just give them a coating of white, for that is as it ought to be; besides, it is good for the oranges and the grapes." And then away she flew, and Kay sat quite alone in the empty halls of ice that were miles long, and looked at the blocks of ice, and thought and thought till his skull was almost cracked. There he sat quite benumbed and motionless; one would have imagined he was frozen to death.

Suddenly little Gerda stepped through the great portal into the palace. The gate was formed of cutting winds; but Gerda repeated her evening prayer, and the winds were laid as though they slept; and the little maiden entered the vast, empty, cold halls. There she beheld Kay: she recognized him, flew to embrace him, and cried out, her arms firmly holding him the while, "Kay, sweet little Kay! Have I then found you at last?"

But he sat quite still, benumbed and cold. Then little Gerda shed burning tears; and they fell on his bosom, they penetrated to his heart, they thawed the lumps of ice, and consumed the splinters of the looking-glass; he looked at her, and she sang the hymn:

"The rose in the valley is blooming so sweet, And angels descend there the children to greet."

Hereupon Kay burst into tears; he wept so much that

the splinter rolled out of his eye, and he recognized her, and shouted, "Gerda, sweet little Gerda! Where have you been so long? And where have I been?" He looked round him. "How cold it is here!" said he. "How empty and cold!" And he held fast by Gerda, who laughed and wept for joy. It was so beautiful, that even the blocks of ice danced about for joy; and when they were tired and laid themselves down, they formed exactly the letters which the Snow Queen had told him to find out; so now he was his own master, and he would have the whole world and a pair of new skates into the bargain.

Gerda kissed his cheeks, and they grew quite blooming; she kissed his eyes, and they shone like her own; she kissed his hands and feet, and he was again well and merry. The Snow Queen might come back as soon as she liked; there stood his discharge written in resplendent masses of ice.

They took each other by the hand, and wandered forth out of the large hall; they talked of their old grandmother, and of the roses upon the roof; and wherever they went, the winds ceased raging, and the sun burst forth. And when they reached the bush with the red berries, they found the Reindeer waiting for them. He had brought another, a young one, with him, whose udder was filled with milk, which he gave to the little ones, and kissed their lips. They then carried Kay and Gerda – first to the Finland woman, where they warmed themselves in the warm room, and learned what they were to do on their journey home; and they went to the Lapland woman, who made some new clothes for them and repaired their sledges.

The Reindeer and the young hind leaped along beside them, and accompanied them to the boundary of the country. Here the first vegetation peeped forth; here Kay and Gerda took leave of the Lapland woman. "Farewell! Farewell!" they all said. And the first green buds appeared, the first little birds began to chirrup; and out of the wood came, riding on a magnificent horse, which Gerda knew (it was one of the leaders in the golden carriage), a young damsel with a bright-red cap on her head, and armed with pistols. It was the little robber maiden, who, tired of being at home, had determined to make a journey to the north; and afterwards in another direction, if that did not please her. She recognized Gerda immediately, and Gerda knew her too. It was a joyful meeting.

"You are a fine fellow for tramping about," said she to little Kay; "I should like to know, faith, if you deserve that one should run from one end of the world to the other for your sake?"

But Gerda patted her cheeks, and inquired for the Prince and Princess.

"They are gone abroad," said the other.

"But the Raven?" asked little Gerda.

"Oh! The Raven is dead," she answered. "His tame sweetheart is a widow, and wears a bit of black worsted round her leg; she laments most piteously, but it's all mere talk and stuff! Now tell me what you've been doing and how you managed to catch him."

And Gerda and Kay both told their story.

And "Schnipp-schnapp-schnurre-basselurre," said the robber maiden; and she took the hands of each, and promised that if she should some day pass through the town where they lived, she would come and visit them; and then away she rode. Kay and Gerda took each other's hand: it was lovely spring weather, with abundance of flowers and of verdure. The church-bells rang, and the children recognized the high towers, and the large town; it was that in which they dwelt. They entered and hastened up to their grandmother's room, where everything was standing as formerly. The clock said "tick! tack!" and the finger moved round; but as they entered, they remarked that they were now grown up. The roses on the leads hung blooming in at the open window; there stood the little children's chairs, and Kay and Gerda sat down on them, holding each other by the hand; they both had forgotten the cold empty splendour of the Snow Queen, as though it had been a dream. The grandmother sat in the bright sunshine, and read aloud from the Bible: "Unless ye become as little children, ye cannot enter the kingdom of heaven."

And Kay and Gerda looked in each other's eyes, and all at once they understood the old hymn:

"The rose in the valley is blooming so sweet, And angels descend there the children to greet."

There sat the two grown-up persons; grown-up, and yet children; children at least in heart; and it was summer-time; summer, glorious summer!